Mystery Ranch

by

Arthur Chapman

Double 9 BOOKS

Mystery Ranch

by Arthur Chapman

ISBN: 978-93-71139-07-6

Published by

DOUBLE 9 BOOKS
2/13-B, Ansari Road
Daryaganj, New Delhi – 110002
info@double9books.com
www.double9books.com
Tel. 011-40042856

ABOUT THE AUTHOR

Arthur Chapman (1880–1935) was an American poet and author known for his works centered around the Western genre. Born in Colorado, Chapman had a deep connection with the American West, which greatly influenced his writing. Chapman's writing is renowned for its vivid portrayal of Western life and landscapes. His works often reflect his firsthand experience and appreciation of the region, capturing the spirit of the frontier and the lives of cowboys and ranchers. In addition to his novels, Chapman was a prolific poet. His poetry often celebrated the Western experience, contributing to his reputation as a key figure in Western literature. His poetic style is noted for its simplicity and authenticity, resonating with readers who appreciate the rugged beauty of the West. One of his best-known works is "Rustlers Beware," a novel that exemplifies his focus on Western adventure and conflict. His other writings include poetry collections and short stories that explore similar themes. Arthur Chapman's contributions to Western literature have left a lasting impact, with his works continuing to be appreciated for their evocative portrayal of the American frontier and its enduring spirit.

CONTENTS

CHAPTER I

There was a swift padding of moccasined feet through the hall leading to the Indian agent's office.

Ordinarily Walter Lowell would not have looked up from his desk. He recognized the footfalls of Plenty Buffalo, his chief of Indian police, but this time there was an absence of the customary leisureliness in the official's stride. The agent's eyes were questioning Plenty Buffalo before the police chief had more than entered the doorway.

The Indian, a broad-shouldered, powerfully built man in a blue uniform, stopped at the agent's desk and saluted. Lowell knew better than to ask him a question at the outset. News speeds best without urging when an Indian tells it. The clerk who acted as interpreter dropped his papers and moved nearer, listening intently as Plenty Buffalo spoke rapidly in his tribal tongue.

"A man has been murdered on the road just off the reservation," announced the interpreter.

Still the agent did not speak.

"I just found him," went on the police chief to the clerk, who interpreted rapidly. "You'd better come and look things over."

"How do you know he was murdered?" asked the agent, reaching for his desk telephone.

"He was shot."

"But couldn't he have shot himself?"

"No. He's staked down."

Lowell straightened up suddenly, a tingle of apprehension running through him. Staked down—and on the edge of the Indian reservation! Matters were being brought close home.

"Is there anything to tell who he is?"

"I didn't look around much," said Plenty Buffalo. "There's an auto in the road. That's what I saw first."

"Where is the body?"

"A few yards from the auto, on the prairie."

The agent called the sheriff's office at White Lodge, the adjoining county seat. The sheriff was out, but Lowell left the necessary information as to the location of the automobile and the body. Then he put on his hat, and, gathering up his gloves, motioned to Plenty Buffalo and the interpreter to follow him to his automobile which was standing in front of the agency office. Plenty Buffalo's pony was left at the hitching-rack, to recover from the hard run it had just been given. The wooden-handled quirt at the saddle had not been spared by the Indian.

Flooded with June sunshine the agency had never looked more attractive, from the white man's standpoint. The main street was wide, with a parkway in the center, shaded with cottonwoods. The school buildings, dormitories, dining-hall, auditorium, and several of the employees' residences faced this street. The agent's house nestled among trees and shrubbery on the most attractive corner. The sidewalks were wide, and made of cement. There was a good water system, as the faithfully irrigated lawns testified. Arc lights swung from the street intersections, and there were incandescents in every house. A sewer system had just been completed. Indian boys and girls were looking after gardens in vacant lots. There were experimental ranches surrounding the agency. In the stables and enclosures were pure-bred cattle and sheep, the nucleus of tribal flocks and herds of better standards.

In less than four years Walter Lowell had made the agency a model of its kind. He had done much to interest even the older Indians in agriculture. The school-children, owing to a more liberal educational system, had lost the customary look of apathy. The agent's work had been commended in annual reports from Washington. The agency had been featured in newspaper and magazine articles, and yet Lowell had felt that he was far from accomplishing anything permanent. Ancient customs and superstitions had to be reckoned with. Smouldering fires occasionally broke out in most alarming fashion. Only recently there had been a serious impairment of reservation morale, owing to the spectacular rise of a young Indian named Fire Bear, who had gathered many followers, and who, with his cohorts, had proceeded to dance and "make medicine" to the exclusion of all other employment. Fire Bear's defection had set many rumors afloat. Timid settlers near the reservation had expressed fear of a general uprising, which fear had been fanned by the threats and boastings sent broadcast by some of Fire Bear's more reckless followers.

Lowell was frankly worried as he sped away from the agency with Plenty Buffalo and the interpreter. Every crime, large or small, which occurred near the reservation, and which did not carry its own solution, was laid to Indians. Here was something which pointed directly to Indian handiwork, and Lowell in imagination could hear a great outcry going up.

Plenty Buffalo gave little more information as the car swayed along the road that led off the reservation.

"He says he was off the reservation trailing Jim McFann," remarked the interpreter. "He thought Jim was going along the road to Talpers's store, but Plenty Buffalo was mistaken. He did not find Jim, but what he did find was this man who had been killed."

"Jim McFann isn't a bad fellow at heart, but this bootlegging and trailing around with Bill Talpers will get him in trouble yet," replied the agent. "He's pretty clever, or Plenty Buffalo's men would have caught him long before this."

They were approaching Talpers's store as the agent spoke. The store was a barn-like building, with a row of poplars at the north, and a big cottonwood in front. A few houses were clustered about. Bill Talpers, storekeeper and postmaster, looked out of the door as the automobile went past. Generally there were Indians sitting in front of the store, but to-day there were none. Plenty Buffalo volunteered the information that there had been a "big sing" on a distant part of the reservation which had attracted most of the residents from this neighborhood. Talpers was seen running out to his horse, which stood in front of the store.

"He'll be along pretty soon," said the agent. "He knows there's something unusual going on."

The road over which the party was traveling was sometimes called the Dollar Sign, for the reason that it wound across the reservation line like a letter S. After leaving White Lodge, which was off the reservation, any traveler on the road crossed the line and soon went through the agency. Then there was a curve which took him across the line again to Talpers's, after which a reverse curve swept back into the Indians' domain. All of which was the cause of no little trouble to the agent and the Indian police, for bootleggers found it easy to operate from White Lodge or Talpers's and drop back again across the line to safety.

Another ten miles, on the sweep of the road toward the reservation, and the automobile was sighted. The body was found, as Plenty Buffalo had described it. The man had been murdered—that much was plain enough.

"Buckshot, from a sawed-off shotgun probably," said the agent, shuddering.

Whoever had fired the shot had done his work with deadly accuracy. Part of the man's face had been carried away. He had been well along in years, as his gray hair indicated, but his frame was sturdy. He was dressed in khaki—a garb much affected by transcontinental automobile tourists. The car which he had been driving was big and expensive.

Other details were forgotten for the moment in the fact that the man had been staked to the prairie. Ropes had been attached to his hands and feet. These ropes were fastened to tent-stakes driven into the prairie.

"The man had been camping along the route," said the agent, "and whoever did this shooting probably used the victim's own tent-stakes."

This opinion was confirmed after a momentary examination of the tonneau of the car, which disclosed a tent, duffle-bag, and other camping equipment.

"Look around the prairie and see if you can find any of this man's belongings scattered about," said Lowell.

"Plenty Buffalo wants to know if you noticed all the pony tracks," said the interpreter.

"Yes," replied Lowell bitterly. "I couldn't very well help seeing them. What does Plenty Buffalo think about them?"

"They're Indian pony tracks—no doubt about that," said the interpreter, "but there is no telling just when they were made."

"I see. It might have been at the time of the murder, or afterward."

Lowell looked closely at the pony tracks, which were thick about the automobile and the body. Plainly there had been a considerable body of horsemen on the scene. Plenty Buffalo, skilled in trailing, had not hesitated to announce that the tracks were those of Indian ponies. If more evidence were needed, there were the imprints of moccasined feet in the dust.

Lowell surveyed the scene while Plenty Buffalo and the interpreter searched the prairie for more clues. The agent did not want to disturb the body nor search the automobile until the arrival of the sheriff, as the murder had happened outside of Government jurisdiction, and the local authorities were jealous of their rights. The murder had been done close to the brow of a low hill. The gently rolling prairie stretched to a creek on one side, and to interminable distance on the other. There was a carpet of green grass in both directions, dotted with clumps of sagebrush. It had rained a few days before—the last rain of many, it chanced—and there were damp spots in the road in places and the grass and the sage were fresh in color. Meadow-larks were trilling, and the whole scene was one of peace—provided the beholder could blot out the memory of the tenantless clay stretched out upon clay.

In a few minutes Sheriff Tom Redmond and a deputy arrived in an automobile from White Lodge. They were followed by Bill Talpers, in the saddle.

Redmond was a tall, square-shouldered cattleman, who still clung to the rough garb and high-heeled boots of the cowpuncher, though he seldom used any means of travel but the automobile. Western winds, heated by fiery Western suns, had burned his face to the color of saddle-leather. His eyebrows were shaggy and light-colored, and Nature's bleaching elements had reduced a straw-colored mustache to a discouraging nondescript tone.

"Looks like an Injun job, Lowell, don't it?" asked Redmond, as his sharp eyes took in the situation in darting glances.

"Isn't it a little early to come to that conclusion?" queried the agent.

"There ain't no other conclusion to come to," broke in Talpers, who had joined the group in an inspection of the scene. "Look at them pony tracks—all Injun."

Talpers was broad—almost squat of figure. His complexion was brick red. He had a thin, curling black beard and mustache. He was one of the men to whom alkali is a constant poison, and his lips were always cracked and bleeding. His voice was husky and disagreeable, his small eyes bespoke the brute in him, and yet he was not without certain qualities of leadership which seemed to appeal particularly to the Indians. His store was headquarters for the rough and idle element of the reservation. Also it was the center of considerable white trade, for it was the only store for miles in either direction, and in addition was the general post-office.

Knowing of Talpers's friendliness for the rebellious element among the Indians, Lowell looked at the trader in surprise.

"You didn't see any Indians doing this, did you, Talpers?" he asked.

The trader hastened to qualify his remark, as it would not do to have the word get out among the Indians that he had attempted to throw the blame on them.

"No—I ain't exactly sayin' that Injuns done it," said the trader, "but I ain't ever seen more signs pointin' in one direction."

"Well, don't let signs get you so far off the right trail that you can't get back again," replied the agent, turning to help Tom Redmond and his deputy in the work of establishing the identity of the slain man.

It was work that did not take long. Papers were found in the pockets indicating that the victim was Edward B. Sargent, of St. Louis. In the automobile was found clothing bearing St. Louis trademarks.

"Judging from the balance in this checkbook," said the sheriff, "he was a man who didn't have to worry about financial affairs. Probably this is only a checking account, for running expenses, but there's thirty thousand to his credit."

"He's probably some tourist on his way to the coast," observed the deputy, "and he thought he'd make a détour and see an Injun reservation.

Somebody saw a good chance for a holdup, but he showed fight and got killed."

"Nobody reported such a machine as going through the agency," offered Lowell. "The car is big enough and showy enough to attract attention anywhere."

"I didn't see him go past my place," said Talpers. "And if my clerk'd seen him he'd have said somethin' about it."

"Well, he was killed sometime yesterday—that's sure," remarked the sheriff. "He might have come through early in the morning and nobody saw him, or he might have hit White Lodge and the agency and Talpers's late at night and camped here along the Dollar Sign until morning and been killed when he started on. The thing of it is that this is as far as he got, and we've got to find the ones that's responsible. This kind of a killing is jest going to make the White Lodge Chamber of Commerce get up on its hind legs and howl. There's bound to be speeches telling how, just when we've about convinced the East that we've shook off our wild Western ways, here comes a murder that's wilder'n anything that's been pulled off since the trapper days."

"Accordin' to my way of thinkin'," said Talpers, "that man wasn't tortured after he was staked down. Any one who knows anything about Injun character knows that when they pegged a victim out that way, they intended for him to furnish some amusement, such as having splinters stuck into him and bein' set afire by the squaws."

"They probably thought they seen some one coming," said the sheriff, "and shot him after they got him tied down, and then made a quick getaway."

"That man was shot before he was tied down," interposed Lowell quietly.

"What makes you think that?" Redmond said quickly.

"There are no powder marks on his face. And any one shot at such close range, by some one standing over him, would have had his head blown away."

Redmond assented, grudgingly.

"What does Plenty Buffalo think about it all?" he asked.

Lowell called the police chief and the interpreter. Plenty Buffalo declared that he was puzzled. He was not prepared to make any statement at all as yet. He might have something later on.

"Very well," said the agent, motioning to Plenty Buffalo to go on with the close investigations he had been silently carrying on. "We may get something of value from him when he has finished looking. But there's no use coaxing him to talk now."

"I s'pose not," rejoined Redmond sneeringly. "What's more, I s'pose he can't even see them Injun pony tracks around the body."

"He called my attention to them as soon as we arrived here," said Lowell. "But as far as that goes he didn't need to. Those things are as evident as the bald fact that the man has been killed."

"Well, that's about the only clue there is, as far as I can figger out," remarked the sheriff testily, "and that points straight and clean to some of your wards on the reservation."

"Count on me for any help," replied Lowell crisply. "All I'm interested in, of course, is seeing the guilty brought out into the light."

Turning away and ending a controversy, which he knew would be fruitless, Lowell made another searching personal examination of the scene. He examined the stakes, having in mind the possibility of finger-prints. But no tell-tale mark had been left behind. The stakes were too rough to admit the possibility of any finger-prints that might be microscopically detected. The road and prairie surrounding the automobile were examined, but nothing save pony tracks, numerous and indiscriminately mingled, rewarded his efforts.

"Them Injuns jest milled around this machine and the body of that hombrey," said Talpers. "There must have been twenty-five of 'em in the bunch, anyway, ain't I right, Plenty Buffalo?" added the trader, repeating his remark in the Indian's tribal tongue, in which the white man was expert.

"Heap Injun here," agreed Plenty Buffalo, not averse to showing off a large part of his limited English vocabulary.

"That trouble-maker, Fire Bear, is the only one who travels much with a gang, ain't he?" demanded Redmond.

"Yes," assented the agent. "He has had from fifty to one hundred young Indians making medicine with him on Wolf Mountain. Rest assured that Fire Bear and every one with him will have to give an account of himself."

"That's the talk!" exclaimed Redmond, pulling at his mustache. "I ain't afraid of your not shooting straight in this thing, Mr. Lowell, but you've got to admit that you've stuck up for Injuns the way no other agent has ever stuck up for 'em before, and natchelly—"

"Naturally you thought I might even cover up murder for them," added Lowell good-naturedly. "Well, get that idea out of your head. But also get it out of your head that I'm going to see any Indian or Indians railroaded for a crime that possibly he or they didn't commit."

"All right!" snapped the sheriff, instantly as belligerent and suspicious as ever. "But this thing is going to be worked out on the evidence, and right now the evidence—"

"Which is all circumstantial."

"Yes, circumstantial it may be, but it's mighty strong against some of your people over that there line, and it's going to be followed up."

Lowell shrugged his shoulders, knowing the futility of further argument with the sheriff, who was representative of the considerable element that always looked upon Indians as "red devils" and that would never admit that any good existed in race or individual.

The agent assisted in removing the body of the murdered man to the big automobile that had been standing in the road, a silent witness to the crime. Lowell drove the machine to White Lodge, at the request of the sheriff, and sent telegrams which might establish the dead man's identity beyond all doubt.

Meantime the news of the murder was not long in making its devious way about the sparsely settled countryside. Most of the population of White Lodge, and ranchers from remote districts, visited the scene. One fortunate individual, who had arrived before the body had been removed, interested various groups by stretching himself out on the prairie on the exact spot where the slain man had been found.

"Here he laid, jest like this," the actor would conclude, "right out here in the bunch grass and prickly pear, with his hands and feet tied to them tent-stakes, and pony tracks and moccasin tracks all mixed around in the dust jest as if a hull tribe had been millin' here. If a lot of Injuns don't swing for this, then there's no use of callin' this a white man's country any more."

The flames of resentment needed no fanning, as Lowell found. The agent had not concluded his work with the sheriff at White Lodge before he heard thinly veiled threats directed at all Indians and their friends. He paid no attention to the comments, but drove back to the agency, successfully masking the grave concern he felt. In the evening, his chief clerk, Ed Rogers, found Lowell reading a magazine.

"The talk is that you'll have to get Fire Bear for this murder," said Rogers. Then the chief clerk added, bluntly: "I thought sure you'd be working on this case."

Lowell smiled at the clerk's astonishment.

"There's nothing more that requires my attention just now," he said. "If Fire Bear is wanted, we can always get him. That's one thing that simplifies all such matters, where Indians are concerned. An Indian can't lose himself in a crowd, like a white man. Furthermore, he never thinks of leaving the reservation."

Here the young agent rose and yawned.

"Anyway," he remarked, "it isn't our move right now. Until it is, I prefer to think of pleasanter things."

But the agent's thoughts were not on any of the pleasant things contained in the magazine he had flung into a corner. They were dwelling most consistently upon a pleasing journey he had enjoyed, a few days before, with a young woman whom he had taken from the agency to Mystery Ranch.

CHAPTER II

Helen Ervin's life in a private school for girls at San Francisco had been uneventful until her graduation. She had been in the school for ten years. Before that, she had vague recollections of a school that was not so well conducted. In fact, almost her entire recollection was of teachers, school chums, and women who had been hired as companions and tutors. Some one had paid much money for her upbringing—that much Helen Ervin knew. The mystery of her caretaking was known, of course, by Miss Scovill, head of the Scovill School, but it had never been disclosed. It had become such an ancient mystery that Helen told herself she had lost all interest in it. Miss Scovill was kind and motherly, and would answer any other questions. She had taken personal charge of the girl, who lived at the Scovill home during vacations as well as throughout the school year.

"Some day it will all be explained to you," Miss Scovill had said, "but for the present you are simply to learn all you can and continue to be just as nice as you have been. And meantime rest assured that somebody is vitally interested in your welfare and happiness."

The illuminating letter came a few days after graduation. The girls had all gone home and school was closed. Helen was alone in the Scovill home. Miss Scovill had gone away for a few days, on business.

The letter bore a postmark with a strange, Indian-sounding name: "White Lodge." It was in a man's handwriting—evidently a man who had written much. The signature, which was first to be glanced at by the girl, read: "From your affectionate stepfather, Willis Morgan." The letter was as follows:

> No doubt you will be surprised at getting this letter from one whose existence you have not suspected. I had thought to let you remain in darkness concerning me. For years I have been pleased to pay your expenses in school—glad in the thought that you were getting the best care and education that could be purchased. But my affairs have taken a bad turn. I am, to put it vulgarly, cramped financially. Moreover, the loneliness in my heart has become fairly overmastering. I can steel myself

> against it no longer. I want you with me in my declining years. I cannot leave here. I have become greatly attached to this part of the country, and have no doubt that you will be, also. Sylvan scenes, with a dash of human savagery in the foreground, form the best relief for a too-extended assimilation of books. It has been like balm to me, and will prove so to you.
>
> Briefly, I want you to come, and at once. A check to cover expenses is enclosed. Your school years are ended, and a life of quiet, amid scenes of aboriginal romance, awaits you here. Selfishly, perhaps, I appeal to your gratitude, if the prospect I have held out does not prove enticing of itself. If what I have done for you in all these years entitles me to any return, I ask you not to delay the payment. By coming now, you can wipe the slate clean of any indebtedness.

Then followed directions about reaching the ranch—the Greek Letter Ranch, the writer called it—and a final appeal to her sense of gratitude.

When Helen finished reading the letter, her heart was suffused with pity for this lonely man who had come thus strangely and unexpectedly into her life. Her good impulses had always prompted her strongly. Miss Scovill was away, so Helen left her a note of explanation, telling everything in detail. "I know, dear foster mother," wrote the girl, "that you are going to rejoice with me, now that I have found my stepfather. I'll be looking forward to the time when you can visit us at the Greek Letter Ranch."

Making ready for the journey took only a short time. In a few hours Helen was on her way, little knowing that Miss Scovill, on her return, was frantically sending out telegrams which indicated anything but a peaceful acceptance of conditions. One of these telegrams, sent to an address which Helen would not have recognized, read:

> The dove has been lured to the serpent's nest. Take what action you deem best, but quickly.

Helen enjoyed her trip through California and then eastward through the Northwest country to the end of the spur which pointed toward the reservation. From the railroad's end she went to White Lodge by stage. From White Lodge she was told she had better take a private conveyance to her destination. She hired a rig of a livery-stable keeper, who said he could not possibly take her beyond the Indian agency.

"Mebbe some one there'll take you the rest of the way," said the liveryman; and, accepting his hopeful view of the situation, the girl consented to go on in such indefinite fashion.

Thus it happened that a slender, white-clad young woman, with a suitcase at her feet, stood on the agency office porch, undergoing the steady scrutiny of four or five blanketed Indian matrons when Walter Lowell came back from lunch. In a few words Helen had explained matters, and Lowell picked up her suitcase, and, after ascertaining that she had had no lunch, escorted her up the street to the dining-hall.

"We have a little lunch club of employees, and guests often sit in with us," said the agent cordially. "After you eat, and have rested up a bit, I'll see that you are driven over to the—to the Greek Letter Ranch."

As a matter of fact, Lowell had to think several times before he could get the Greek Letter Ranch placed in his mind. He had fallen into the habit—in common with others in the neighborhood—of calling it Mystery Ranch. Also Willis Morgan's name was mentioned so seldom that the agent's mental gymnastics were long sustained and almost painfully apparent before he had matters righted.

"Rogers," said Lowell to his chief clerk, on getting back to the agency office, "how many years has Willis Morgan been in this part of the country?"

"Willis Morgan," echoed Rogers, scratching his head. "Oh, I know now! You mean the 'squaw professor.' He hasn't been called Morgan since he married that squaw who died five years go. There was talk that he used to be a college professor, which is right, I guess, from the number of books he reads. But when he married an Indian folks just called him the 'squaw prof.' He's been out here twelve or fifteen years, I guess. Let's see—he got those Indian lands through his wife when Jones was agent. He must have moved off the reservation when Arbuckle was agent, just before you came on."

"Did he always use a Greek letter brand on his cattle?"

"Always. He never ran many cattle. I guess he hasn't got any at all now. But what he did have he always insisted on having branded with that pitchfork brand, as the cowpunchers call it."

"I know—it's the letter Psi."

"Well, Si, or whatever other nickname it is, even the toughest-hearted old cowmen used to kick on having to put such a big brand on critters. That big pitchfork on flanks or shoulders must have spoiled many a hide for Morgan, but he always insisted on having it slapped on."

"Have the Indians always got along with him pretty well?"

"Yes, because they're afraid of him and leave him alone. It ain't physical fear, but something deeper, like being afraid of a snake, I guess. You see he knows so damn much, he's uncanny. It's the power of mind over matter. Seems funny to think of him having the biggest Indians buffaloed, but he's done it, and he's buffaloed the white folks, too. He gave it out that he wanted to be let alone, and, by jimminy, he's been let alone! I'll bet there aren't four people in the county who have seen his face in as many years."

"Did he have any children?"

"No. His wife was a pretty little Indian woman. He just married her to show his defiance of society, I guess. Anyway, he must have killed her by inches. If he had the other Indians scared, you can imagine how he must have terrorized her. Yet I'll bet he never raised his voice above an ordinary conversational tone."

Lowell frowned as he looked out across the agency street.

"Why, what's come up about Morgan?" asked Rogers.

"Oh, not such a lot," replied the agent. "It's only that there's a girl here—his stepdaughter, it seems—and she's going to make her home with him."

"Good Lord!" ejaculated the chief clerk.

"She's over at the club table now having lunch," went on Lowell. "I'm going to drive her over to the ranch. She seems to think this stepfather of hers is all kinds of a nice fellow, and I can't tell her that she'd better take her little suitcase and go right back where she came from. Besides, who knows that she may be right and we've been misjudging Morgan all these years?"

"Well, if Willis Morgan's been misjudged, then I'm really an angel all ready to sprout wings," observed the clerk. "But maybe he's braced up, or, if he hasn't, this stepdaughter has tackled the job of reforming him. If she does it, it'll be the supreme test of what woman can do along that line."

"What business have bachelors such as you and I to be talking about any reformations wrought by woman?" asked Lowell smilingly.

"Not much," agreed Rogers. "Outside of the school-teachers and other agency employees I haven't seen a dozen white women since I went to Denver three years ago. And you—why, you haven't been away from here except on one trip to Washington in the last four years."

Each man looked out of the window, absorbed in his own dreams. Lowell had forsaken an active career to take up the routine of an Indian agent's life. After leaving college he had done some newspaper work, which he abandoned because a position as land investigator for a corporation with oil interests in view had given him a chance to travel in the West. There had been a chance journey across an Indian reservation, with a sojourn at an agency. Lowell had decided that his work had been spread before him. By persistent personal effort and the use of some political influence, he secured an appointment as Indian agent. The monetary reward was small, but he had not regretted his choice. Only there were memories such as this girl brought to him—memories of college days when there were certain other girls in white dresses, and when there was music far removed from weird Indian chants, and the thud-thud of moccasins was not always in his ears....

Lowell rose hastily.

"They must be through eating over there," he said. "But I positively hate to start the trip that will land the girl at that ranch."

The agent drove his car over to the dining-hall. When Helen came out, the agency blacksmith was carrying her suitcase, and the matron, Mrs. Ryers, had her arm about the girl's waist, for friends are quickly made in the West's lonely places. School-teachers and other agency employees chorused good-bye as the automobile was driven away.

The girl was flushed with pleasure, and there were tears in her eyes.

"I don't blame you for liking to live on an Indian reservation," she said, "amid such cordial people."

"Well, it isn't so bad, though, of course, we're in a backwater here," said Lowell. "An Indian reservation gives you a queer feeling that way. The tides of civilization are racing all around, but here the progress is painfully slow."

"Tell me more about it, please," pleaded the girl. "This lovely place—surely the Indians like it."

"Some of them do, perhaps," said Lowell. "But they haven't been trained to this sort of thing. A lodge out there on the prairie, with game to be hunted and horses to be ridden—that would suit the most advanced of them better than settled life anywhere. But, of course, all that is impossible, and the thing is to reconcile them to the inevitable things they have to face. And even reconciling white people to the inevitable is no easy job."

"No, it's harder, really, than teaching these poor Indians, I suppose," agreed the girl. "But don't you find lots to recompense you?"

Lowell stole a look at her, and then he slowed the car's pace considerably. There was no use hurrying to the ranch with such a charming companion aboard. The fresh June breeze had loosened a strand or two of her brown hair. The bright, strong sunshine merely emphasized the youthful perfection of her complexion. She had walked with a certain buoyancy of carriage which Lowell ascribed to athletics. Her eyes were brown, and rather serious of expression, but her smile was quick and natural—the sort of a smile that brings one in return, so Lowell concluded in his fragmentary process of cataloguing. Her youth was the splendid thing about her to-day. To-morrow her strong, resourceful womanhood might be still more splendid. Lowell surrendered himself completely to the enjoyment of the drive, and likewise he slowed down the car another notch.

"Of course, just getting out of school, I haven't learned so much about the inevitableness of life," said the girl, harking back to Lowell's remark concerning the Indians, "but I'm beginning to sense the responsibilities now. I've just learned that it was my stepfather who kept me in that delightful school so many years, and now it's time for repayment."

"Repayment seems to be exacted for everything in life," said Lowell automatically, though he was too much astonished at the girl's remark to tell whether his reply had been intelligible. Was it possible the "squaw professor" had been misjudged all these years, and was living a life of sacrifice in order that this girl might have every opportunity? Lowell had not recovered from the astounding idea before they reached Talpers's place. He stopped the automobile in front of the store, and the trader came out.

"Mr. Talpers, meet Miss Ervin, daughter of our neighbor, Mr. Morgan," said the agent. "Miss Ervin will probably be coming over here after her mail, and you might as well meet her now."

Talpers bobbed his head, but not enough to break the stare he had bent upon the girl, who flushed under his scrutiny. As a matter of fact, the trader had been too taken aback at the thought of a woman—and a young and pretty woman—being related to the owner of Mystery Ranch to do more than mumble a greeting. Then the vividness of the girl's beauty had slowly worked upon him, rendering his speechlessness absolute.

"I don't like Mr. Talpers as well as I do some of your Indians," said the girl, as they rolled away from the store, leaving the trader on the platform, still staring.

"Well, I don't mind confiding in you, as I've confided in Bill himself, that Mr. Talpers is something over ninety per cent undesirable. He is one of the thorns that grow expressly for the purpose of sticking in the side of Uncle Sam. He's cunning and dangerous, and constantly lowers the reservation morale, but he's over the line and I can't do a thing with him unless I get him red-handed. But he's postmaster and the only trader near here, and you'll have to know him, so I thought I'd bring out the Talpers exhibit early."

Helen laughed, and forgot her momentary displeasure as the insistent appeal of the landscape crowded everything else from her mind. The white road lay like a carelessly flung thread on the billowing plateau land. The air was crisp with the magic of the upper altitudes. Gray clumps of sagebrush stood forth like little islands in the sea of grass. A winding line of willows told where a small stream lay hidden. The shadows of late afternoon were filling distant hollows with purple. Remote mountains broke the horizon in a serrated line. Prairie flowers scented the snow-cooled breeze.

They paused on the top of a hill, where, a few days later, a tragedy was to be enacted. The agent said nothing, letting the panorama tell its own story.

"Oh, it's almost overwhelming," said Helen finally, with a sigh. "Sometimes it all seems so intimate, and personally friendly, and then those meadow-larks stop singing for a moment, and the sun brings out the bigness of everything—and you feel afraid, or at least I do."

Lowell smiled understandingly.

"It works on strong men the same way," he said. "That's why there are no Indian tramps, I guess. No Indian ever went 'on his own' in this big country. The tribes people always clung together. The white trappers came and tried life alone, but lots of them went queer as a penalty. The cowpunchers flocked together and got along all right, but many a sheepherder who has tried it alone has had to be taken in charge by his folks. Human companionship out in all those big spaces is just as necessary as bacon, flour, and salt."

The girl sighed wistfully.

"Of course, I've had lots of companionship at school," she said. "Is there any one besides my stepfather on his ranch? There must be, I imagine."

"There's a Chinese cook, I believe—Wong," replied Lowell. "But you are going to find lots to interest you. Besides, if you will let me—"

"Yes, I'll let you drive over real often," laughed the girl, as Lowell hesitated. "I'll be delighted, and I know father will be, also."

Lowell wanted to turn the car around and head it away from the hated ranch which was now so close at hand. His heart sank, and he became silent as they dropped into the valley and approached the watercourse, near which Willis Morgan's cabin stood.

"Here's the place," he said briefly, as he turned into a travesty of a front yard and halted beside a small cabin, built of logs and containing not more than three or four rooms.

The girl looked at Lowell in surprise. Something in the grim set of his jaw told her the truth. Pride came instantly to her rescue, and in a steady voice she made some comment on the quaintness of the surroundings.

There was no welcome—not even the barking of a dog. Lowell took the suitcase from the car, and, with the girl standing at his side, knocked at the heavy pine door, which opened slowly. An Oriental face peered forth. In the background Lowell could see the shadowy figure of Willis Morgan. The man's pale face and gray hair looked blurred in the half-light of the cabin. He did not step to the door, but his voice came, cold and cutting.

"Bring in the suitcase, Wong," said Morgan. "Welcome to this humble abode, stepdaughter o' mine. I had hardly dared hope you would take such a plunge into the primitive."

The girl was trying to voice her gratitude to Lowell when Morgan's hand was thrust forth and grasped hers and fairly pulled her into the doorway. The door closed, and Lowell turned back to his automobile, with anger and pity struggling within him for adequate expression.

CHAPTER III

Walter Lowell tore the wrapper of his copy of the "White Lodge Weekly Star" when the agency mail was put on his desk a few days after the murder on the Dollar Sign road.

"I'm betting Editor Jay Travers cuts into the vitriol supply for our benefit in this issue of his household journal," remarked the agent to his chief clerk.

"He won't overlook the chance," replied Rogers. "Here's where he earns a little of the money the stockmen have been putting into his newspaper during the last few years."

"Yes, here it is: 'Crime Points to Indians. Automobile Tourist Killed Near Reservation. Staked Down, Probably by Redskins. Wave of Horror Sweeping the County—Dancing should be Stopped—Policy of Coddling Indians—White Settlers not Safe.' Oh, take it and read it in detail!" And Lowell tossed the paper to Rogers.

"And right here, where you'd look for it first thing—right at the top of the editorial column—is a regular old-fashioned English leader, calling on the Government to throw open the reservation to grazing," said Rogers.

"The London 'Times' could thunder no more strongly in proportion. The grateful cowmen should throw at least another five thousand into ye editor's coffers. But, after all, what does it matter? A dozen newspapers couldn't make the case look any blacker for the Indians. If some hot-headed white man doesn't read this and take a shot at the first Indian he meets, no great harm will be done."

The inquest over the slain man had been duly held at White Lodge. The coroner's jury found that the murder had been done "by a person or persons unknown." The telegrams which Lowell had sent had brought back the information that Edward B. Sargent was a retired inventor of mining machinery—that he was prosperous, and lived alone. His servants said he had departed in an automobile five days before. He had left no word as to his destination, but had drawn some money from the bank—sufficient to cover expenses on an extended trip. His servants said he was in the habit of taking such trips alone. Generally he went to the Rocky Mountains in his automobile every summer. He was accustomed to life in the open and generally carried a camping outfit. His description tallied with that which had been sent. He had left definite instructions with a trust company about the disposal of his fortune, and about his burial, in case of his death. Would the county authorities at White Lodge please forward remains without delay?

While the inquiry was in progress, Walter Lowell spent much of his time at White Lodge, and caught the brunt of the bitter feeling against the Indians. It seemed as if at least three out of four residents of the county had mentally tried and convicted Fire Bear and his companions.

"And if there is one out of the four that hasn't told me his opinion," said Lowell to the sheriff, "it's because he hasn't been able to get to town."

Sheriff Tom Redmond, though evidently firm in his opinion that Indians were responsible for the crime, was not as outspoken in his remarks as he had been at the scene of the murder. The county attorney, Charley Dryenforth, a young lawyer who had been much interested in the progress of the Indians, had counseled less assumption on the sheriff's part.

"Whoever did this," said the young attorney, "is going to be found, either here in this county or on the Indian reservation. It wasn't any chance job—the work of a fly-by-night tramp or yeggman. The Dollar Sign is too far off the main road to admit of that theory. It's a home job, and the truth will come out sooner or later, just as Lowell says, and the only sensible thing is to work with the agent and not against him—at least until he gives some just cause for complaint."

Like the Indian agent, the attorney had a complete understanding of the prejudices in the case. There is always pressure about any Indian reservation. White men look across the line at unfenced acres, and complain bitterly against a policy that gives so much land to so few individuals. There are constant appeals to Congressmen. New treaties, which disregard old covenants as scraps of paper, are constantly being introduced. Leasing laws are being made and remade and fought over. The Indian agent is the local buffer between contending forces. But, used as he was to unfounded complaint and criticism, Walter Lowell was hardly prepared for the bitterness that descended upon him at White Lodge after the crime on the Dollar Sign. Men with whom he had hunted and fished, cattlemen whom he had helped on the round-up, and storekeepers whose trade he had swelled to considerable degree, attempted to engage in argument tinged with acrimony. Lowell attempted to answer a few of them at first, but saw how futile it all was, and took refuge in silence. He waited until there was nothing more for him to do at White Lodge, and then he went back to the agency to complete the job of forgetting an incredible number of small personal injuries.... There was the girl at Willis Morgan's ranch. Surely she would be outside of all these wave-like circles of distrust and rancor. He intended to have gone to see her within a day or two after he had taken her over to Morgan's, but something insistent had come up at the agency, and then had come the murder. Well, he would go over right away. He took his hat and gloves and started for the automobile, when the telephone rang.

"It's Sheriff Tom Redmond," said Rogers. "He's coming over to see you about going out after Fire Bear. An indictment's been found, and he's bringing a warrant charging Fire Bear with murder."

Bill Talpers sat behind the letter cage that marked off Uncle Sam's corner of his store, and paid no attention to the waiting Indian outside who wanted a high-crowned hat, but who knew better than to ask for it.

Being postmaster had brought no end of problems to Bill. This time it was a problem that was not displeasing, though Mr. Talpers was not quite sure as yet how it should be followed out. The problem was contained in a letter which Postmaster Bill held in his hand. The letter was open, though it was not addressed to the man who had read it a dozen times and who was still considering its import.

Lovingly, Bill once more looked at the address on the envelope. It was in a feminine hand and read:

> MR. EDWARD B. SARGENT.

The town that figured on the envelope was Quaking-Asp Grove, which was beyond White Lodge, on the main transcontinental highway. Slowly Bill took from the envelope a note which read:

> *Dear Uncle and Benefactor*:
>
> I have learned all. Do not come to the ranch for me, as you have planned. Evil impends. In fact I feel that he means to do you harm. I plead with you, do not come. It is the only way you can avert certain tragedy. I am sending this by Wong, as I am watched closely, though he pretends to be looking out only for my welfare. I can escape in some way. I am not afraid—only for you. Again I plead with you not to come. You will be going into a deathtrap.
>
> Helen

Wong, the factotum from the Greek Letter Ranch, had brought the letter and had duly stamped it and dropped it in the box for outgoing mail, three days before the murder on the Dollar Sign road. Wong had all the appearance of a man frightened and in a hurry. Talpers sought to detain him, but the Chinese hurried back to his old white horse and climbed clumsily into the saddle.

"It's a long time sence I've seen that old white hoss with the big pitchfork brand on his shoulder," said Talpers. "You ain't ridin' up here for supplies as often as you used to, Wong. Must be gettin' all your stuff by mail-order route. Well, I ain't sore about it, so wait awhile and have a little smoke and talk."

But Wong had shaken his head and departed as rapidly in the direction of the ranch as his limited riding ability would permit.

The letter that Wong had mailed had not gone to its addressed destination. Talpers had opened it and read it, out of idle curiosity, intending to seal the flap again and remail it if it proved to be nothing out of the ordinary. But there were hints of interesting things in the letter, and Bill kept it a day or so for re-reading. Then he kept it for another day because he had stuck it in his pocket and all but forgotten about it. Afterward came the murder, with the name of Sargent figuring, and Bill kept the letter for various reasons, one of which was that he did not know what else to do with it.

"It's too late for that feller to git it now, any ways," was Bill's comfortable philosophy. "And if I'd go and mail it now, some fool inspector might make it cost me my job as postmaster. Besides, it may come useful in my business—who knows?"

The usefulness of the letter, from Bill's standpoint, began to be apparent the day after the murder, when Helen Ervin rode up to the store on the white horse which Wong had graced. The girl rode well. She was hatless and dressed in a neat riding-suit—the conventional attire of her classmates who had gone in for riding-lessons. Her riding-clothes were the first thing she had packed, on leaving San Francisco, as the very word "ranch" had suggested delightful excursions in the saddle.

Two or three Indians sat stolidly on the porch as Helen rode up. She had learned that the old horse was not given to running away. He might roll, to rid himself of the flies, but he was not even likely to do that with the saddle on, so Helen did not trouble to tie him to the rack. She let the reins drop to the ground and walked past the Indians into the store, where Bill Talpers was watching her greedily from behind his postmaster's desk.

"You are postmaster here, Mr. Talpers, aren't you?" asked Helen, with a slight acknowledgment of the trader's greeting.

Bill admitted that Uncle Sam had so honored him.

"I'm looking for a letter that was mailed here by Wong, and should be back from Quaking-Asp Grove by this time. It had a return address on it, and I understand the person to whom it was sent did not receive it."

Talpers leaned forward mysteriously and fixed his animal-like gaze on Helen.

"I know why he didn't git it," said Bill. "He didn't git it because he was murdered."

Helen turned white, and her riding-whip ceased its tattoo on her boot. She grasped at the edge of the counter for support, and Bill smiled triumphantly. He had played a big card and won, and now he was going to let this girl know who was master.

"There ain't no use of your feelin' cut up," he went on. "If you and me jest understand each other right, there ain't no reason why any one else should know about that letter."

"You held it up and it never reached Quaking-Asp Grove!" exclaimed Helen. "You're the real murderer. I can have you put in prison for tampering with the mails."

The last shot did not make Bill blink. He had been looking for it.

"Ye-es, you might have me put in prison. I admit that," he said, stroking his sparse black beard, "but you ain't goin' to, because I'd feel in duty bound to say that I jest held up the letter in the interests of justice, and turn the hull thing over to the authorities. Old Fussbudget Tom Redmond is jest achin' to make an arrest in this case. He wants to throw the hull Injun reservation in jail, but he'd jest as soon switch to a white person, if confronted with the proper evidence. Now this here letter"—and here Bill took the missive from his pocket—"looks to me like air-tight, iron-bound, copper-riveted sort of testimony that says its own say. Tom couldn't help but act on it, and act quick."

Helen looked about despairingly. The Indians sat like statues on the porch. They had not even turned their heads to observe what was going on inside the store. The old white horse was switching and stamping and shuddering in his constant and futile battle against flies. Beyond the road was silence and prairie.

Turning toward the trader, Helen thought to start in on a plea for mercy, but one look into Talpers's face made her change her mind. Anger set her heart beating tumultuously. She snatched at the letter in the trader's hand, but Bill merely caught her wrist in his big fingers. Swinging the riding-whip with all her strength, she struck Talpers across the face again and again, but he only laughed, and finally wrenched the whip away from her and threw it out in the middle of the floor. Then he released her wrist.

"You've got lots o' spunk," said Bill, coming out from behind the counter, "but that ain't goin' to git you anywheres in pertic'ler in a case like this. You'd better set down on that stool and think things over and act more human."

Helen realized the truth of Talpers's words. Anger was not going to get her anywhere. The black events of recent hours had brought out resourcefulness which she never suspected herself of having. Fortunately

Miss Scovill had been the sort to teach her something of the realities of life. The Scovill School for Girls might have had a larger fashionable patronage if it had turned out more graduates of the clinging-vine type of femininity instead of putting independence of thought and action as among the first requisites.

"That letter doesn't amount to so much as you think," said Helen; "and, anyway, suppose I swear on the stand that I never wrote it?"

"You ain't the kind to swear to a lie," replied Bill, and Helen flushed. "Besides, it's in your writin', and your name's there, and your Chinaman brought it here. You can't git around them things."

"Suppose I tell my stepfather and he comes here and takes the letter away from you?"

Talpers sneered.

"He couldn't git that letter away from me, onless we put it up as a prize in a Greek-slingin' contest. Besides, he's too ornery to help out even his own kin. Why, I ain't one tenth as bad as that stepfather of yourn. He just talked poison into the ears of that Injun wife of his until she died. I guess mebbe by your looks you didn't know he had an Injun wife, but he did. Since she died—killed by inches—he's had that Chinaman doin' the work around the ranch-house. I guess he can't make a dent on the Chinese disposition, or he'd have had Wong dead before this. If you stay there any time at all, he'll have you in an insane asylum or the grave. That's jest the nature of the beast."

Talpers was waxing eloquent, because it had come to him that his one great mission in life was to protect this fine-looking girl from the cruelty of her stepfather. An inexplicable feeling crept into his heart—the first kindly feeling he had ever known.

"It's a dum shame you didn't have any real friends like me to warn you off before you hit that ranch," went on Bill. "That young agent who drove you over ought to have told you, but all he can think of is protectin' Injuns. Now with me it's different. I like Injuns all right, but white folks comes first—especially folks that I'm interested in. Now you and me—"

Helen picked up her riding-whip.

"I can't hear any more to-day," she said.

Talpers followed her through the door and out on the porch.

"All right," he remarked propitiatingly. "This letter'll keep, but mebbe not very long."

In spite of her protests, he turned the horse around for her, and held her stirrup while she mounted. His solicitousness alarmed her more than positive enmity on his part.

"By gosh! you're some fine-lookin' girl," he said admiringly, his gaze sweeping over her neatly clad figure. "There ain't ever been a ridin'-rig like that in these parts. I sure get sick of seein' these squaws bobbin' along on their ponies. There's lots of women around here that can ride, but I never knowed before that the clothes counted so much. Now you and me—"

Helen struck the white horse with her whip. As if by accident, the lash whistled close to Bill Talpers's face, making him give back a step in surprise. As the girl rode away, Talpers looked after her, grinning.

"Some spirited girl," he remarked. "And I sure like spirit. But mebbe this letter I've got'll keep her tamed down a little. Hey, you Bear-in-the-Cloud and Red Star and Crane—you educated sons o' guns settin' around here as if you didn't know a word of English—there ain't any spirits fermentin' on tap to-day, not a drop. It's gettin' scarce and the price is goin' higher. Clear out and wait till Jim McFann comes in to-morrow. He may be able to find somethin' that'll cheer you up!"

CHAPTER IV

Sheriff Tom Redmond was a veteran of many ancient cattle trails. He had traveled as many times from Texas to the Dodge City and Abilene points of shipment as some of our travelers to-day have journeyed across the Atlantic—and he thought just as little about it. More than once he had made the trifling journey from the Rio Grande to Montana, before the inventive individual who supplied fences with teeth had made such excursions impossible. Sheriff Tom had seen many war-bonneted Indians looming through the dust of trail herds. Of the better side of the Indian he knew little, nor cared to learn. But at one time or another he had had trouble with Apache, Comanche, Kiowa, Ute, Pawnee, Arapahoe, Cheyenne, and Sioux. He could tell just how many steers each tribe had cost his employers, and how many horses were still charged off against Indians in general.

"I admit some small prejudice," said Sheriff Tom in the course of one of his numerous arguments with Walter Lowell. "When I see old Crane hanging around Bill Talpers's store, he looks to me jest like the cussed Comanche that rose right out of nowheres and scared me gray-headed when I was riding along all peaceful-like on the Picketwire. And that's the way it goes. Every Injun I see, big or little, resembles some redskin I had trouble with, back in early days. The only thing I can think of 'em doing is shaking buffalo robes and running off live stock—not raising steers to sell. I admit I'm behind the procession. I ain't ready yet to take my theology or my false teeth from an Injun preacher or dentist."

Lowell preferred Sheriff Tom's outspokenness to other forms of opposition and criticism which were harder to meet.

"Some day," he said to the sheriff, "you'll fall in line, but meantime if you can get rid of a pest like Bill Talpers for me, you'll do more for the Indians than they could get out of all the new leases that might be written."

"I've been working on Bill Talpers now for ten years and I ain't been able to git him to stick foot in a trap," was the sheriff's reply. "But I think he's getting to a point where he's all vain-like over the cunning he's shown, and he'll cash himself in, hoss and beaver, when he ain't expecting to."

When the sheriff arrived at the agency, with the warrant for Fire Bear in his pocket, he found a string of saddle and pack animals tied in front of the office, under charge of two of the best cowmen on the reservation, White Man Walks and Many Coups.

"I'll have your car put in with mine, Tom," said Lowell, who was dressed in cowpuncher attire, even to leather *chaparejos*. "I know you're always prepared for riding. There's a saddle horse out there for you. We've some grub and a tent and plenty of bedding, as we may be out several days and find some rough going."

"I judge it ain't going to be any moonlight excursion on the Hudson, then, bringing in this Injun," observed Redmond.

Lowell motioned to the sheriff to step into the private office.

"Affairs are a little complicated," said the agent, closing the door. "Plenty Buffalo has turned up something that makes it look as if Jim McFann may know something about the murder."

"What's Plenty Buffalo found?"

"He discovered a track made by a broken shoe in that conglomeration of hoof marks at the scene of the murder."

"Why didn't he say so at the time?"

"Because he wasn't sure that it pointed to Jim McFann. But he'd been trailing McFann for bootlegging and was pretty sure Jim was riding a horse with a broken shoe. He got hold of an Indian we can trust—an Indian who stands pretty well with McFann—and had him hunt till he found Jim."

"Where was he?"

"McFann was hiding away up in the big hills. What made him light out there no one knows. That looked bad on the face of it. Then this Indian scout of ours, when he happened in on Jim's camp, found that McFann was riding a horse with a broken shoe."

"Looks as if we ought to bring in the half-breed, don't it?"

"Wait a minute. The broken shoe isn't all. Those pieces of rope that were used to tie that man to the stakes—they were cut from a rawhide lariat."

"And Jim McFann uses that kind?"

"Yes."

"Do you know where McFann is hanging out?"

"He may have moved camp, but we can find him."

The sheriff frowned. Matters were getting more complicated than he had thought possible. From the first he had entertained only one idea concerning the murder—that Fire Bear had done the work, or that some of the reckless spirits under the rebellious youth had slain in a moment of bravado.

"Well, it may be that McFann and Fire Bear's crowd had throwed in together and was all mixed up in the killing," remarked the sheriff. "A John Doe warrant ought to be enough to get everybody we want."

"We can get anybody that's wanted," said Lowell, "but you must remember one thing—you're dealing with people who are not used to legal procedure and who may resent wholesale arrests."

"You'll take plenty of Injun police along, I suppose."

"No—I'm not even going to take Plenty Buffalo. The whole police force and all the deputies you might be able to swear in in a week couldn't bring in Fire Bear if he gave the signal to the young fellows around him. We're going alone, except for those two Indians out there, who will just look after camp affairs for us."

"I dunno but you're right," observed Redmond after a pause, during which he keenly scrutinized the young agent's face. "Anyway, I ain't going to let it be said that you've got more nerve than I have. Let the lead hoss go where he chooses—I'll follow the bell."

"Another thing," said Lowell. "You're on an Indian reservation. These Indians have been looking to me for advice and other things in the last four years. If it comes to a point where decisive action has to be taken—"

"You're the one to take it," interrupted the sheriff. "From now on it's your funeral. I don't care what methods you use, so long as I git Fire Bear, and mebbe this half-breed, behind the bars for a hearing down at White Lodge."

The men walked out of the office, and the sheriff was given his mount. The Indians swung the pack-horses into line, and the men settled themselves in their saddles as they began the long, plodding journey to the blue hills in the heart of the reservation.

The lodges of Fire Bear and his followers were placed in a circle, in a grove somber enough for Druidical sacrifice. White cliffs stretched high above the camp, with pine-trees growing at all angles from the interstices of rock. At the foot of the cliffs, and on the green slope that stretched far below to the forest of lodgepole pines, stood many conical, tent-like formations of rock. They were even whiter than the canvas tepees which were grouped in front of them. At any time of the day these formations were uncanny. In time of morning or evening shadow the effect upon the imagination was intensified. The strange outcropping was repeated nowhere else. It jutted forth, white and mysterious—a monstrous tenting-ground left over from the Stone Age. As if to deepen the effect of the weird stage setting, Nature contrived that all the winds which blew here should blow mournfully.

The lighter breezes stirred vague whisperings in the pine-trees. The heavy winds wrought weird noises which echoed from the cliffs.

Lowell had looked upon the Camp of the Stone Tepees once before. There had been a chase for a cattle thief. It was thought he had hidden somewhere in the vicinity of the white semicircle, but he had not been found there, because no man in fear of pursuit could dwell more than a night in so ghostly a place of solitude.

It had been late evening when Lowell had first seen the Camp of the Stone Tepees. He remembered the half-expectant way in which he had paused, thinking to see a white-clad priest emerge from one of the shadowy stone tents and place a human victim upon one of the sacrificial tablets in the open glade. It was early morning when Lowell looked on the scene a second time. He and the sheriff had made a daylight start, leaving the Indians to follow with the pack-horses. It was a long climb up the slopes, among the pines, from the plains below. The trail, for the greater part of the way, had followed a stream which was none too easy fording at the best, and which regularly rose several inches every afternoon owing to the daily melting of late snows in the mountain heights. It was necessary to cross and recross the stream many times. Occasionally the horses floundered over smooth rocks and were nearly carried away. All four men were wet to the waist. Redmond, with memories of countless wider and more treacherous fords crowding upon him, merely jested at each new buffeting in the stream. The Indians were concerned only lest some pack-animal should fall in midstream. Lowell, a good horseman and tireless mountaineer, counted physical discomfort as nothing when such vistas of delight were being opened up.

The giant horseshoe in the cliffs was in semi-darkness when they came in sight of it. Lowell was in the lead, and he turned his horse and motioned to the sheriff to remain hidden in the trees that skirted the glade. The voice of a solitary Indian was flung back and forth in the curve of the cliffs. His back was toward the white men. If he heard them, he made no sign. He was wrapped in a blanket, from shoulders to heels, and was in the midst of a long incantation, flung at the beetling walls with their foot fringe of stone tents. The tepees of the Indians were hardly distinguishable from those which Nature had pitched on this world-old camping-ground. No sound came from the tents of the Indians. Probably the "big medicine" of the Indian was being listened to, but those who heard made no sign.

"It's Fire Bear," said Lowell, as the voice went on and the echoes fluttered back from the cliffs.

"He's sure making big medicine," remarked the sheriff. "They've picked one grand place for a camp. By the Lord! it even sort of gave me the shivers when I first looked at it. What'll we do?"

"Wait till he gets through," cautioned Lowell. "They'd come buzzing out of those tents like hornets if we broke in now, in all probability."

The sheriff's face hardened.

"Jest the same, that sort of thing ought to be stopped—all of it," he said.

"Do you stop every fellow that mounts a soap box, or, what's more likely, stands up on a street corner in an automobile and makes a Socialist speech?"

"No—but that's different."

"Why is it? An Indian reservation is just like a little nation. It has its steady-goers, and it has its share of the shiftless, and also it has an occasional Socialist, and once in a while a rip-snorting Anarchist. Fire Bear doesn't know just what he is yet. He's made some pretty big medicine and made some prophecies that have come true and have gained him a lot of followers, but I can't see that it's up to me to stop him. Not that I have any cause to love that Indian over there in that blanket. He's been the cause of a lot of trouble. He's young and arrogant. In a big city he would be a gang-leader. The police and the courts would find him a problem—and he's just as much, or perhaps more, of a problem out here in the wilds than he would be in town."

The sheriff made no reply, but watched Fire Bear narrowly. Soon the Indian ended his incantations, and the tents of his followers began opening and blanketed figures came forth. Lowell and the sheriff stepped out into the glade and walked toward the camp. The Indians grouped themselves about Fire Bear. There was something of defiance in their attitude, but the white men walked on unconcernedly, and, without any preliminaries, Lowell told Fire Bear the object of their errand.

"You're suspected of murdering that white man on the Dollar Sign road," said Lowell. "You and these young fellows with you were around there. Now you're wanted, to go to White Lodge and tell the court just what you know about things."

Fire Bear was one of the best-educated of the younger generation of Indians. He had carried off honors at an Eastern school, both in his studies and athletics. But his haunts had been the traders' stores when he returned to the reservation. Then he became possessed of the idea that he was a medicine man. Fervor burned in his veins and fired his speech. The young fellows who had idled with him became his zealots. He began making prophecies which mysteriously worked out. He had prophesied a flood, and one came, sweeping away many lodges. When he and his followers were out of food, he had prophesied that plenty would come to them that day. It so happened that lightning that morning struck the trace chain on a load of wood that was being hauled down the mountain-side by a white leaser. The four oxen drawing the load were killed, and the white man gave the beef to the Indians, on condition that they would remove the hides for him. This had sent Fire Bear's stock soaring and had gained many recruits for his camp—even some of the older Indians joining.

Lowell had treated Fire Bear leniently—too leniently most of the white men near the reservation had considered. With the Indians' religious ceremonials had gone the usual dancing. An inspector from Washington had sent in a recommendation that the dancing be stopped at once. Lowell had received several broad hints, following the inspector's letter, but he was waiting an imperative order before stopping the dancing, because he knew that any high-handed interference just then would undo an incalculable amount of his painstaking work with the Indians. He had figured that he could work personally with Fire Bear after the young medicine man's first ardor in his new calling had somewhat cooled. Then had come the murder, with everything pointing to the implication of the young Indian, and with consequent action forced on the agent.

A threatening circle surrounded the white men in Fire Bear's camp.

"Why didn't you bring the Indian police to arrest me?" asked the young Indian leader.

"Because I thought you'd see things in their right light and come," said Lowell.

Fire Bear thought a moment.

"Well, because you did not bring the police, I will go with you," he said.

"You don't have to tell us anything that might be used against you," said the sheriff.

Fire Bear smiled bitterly.

"I've studied white man's law," he said.

Redmond rubbed his head in bewilderment. Such words, coming from a blanketed Indian, in such primitive surroundings, passed his comprehension. Yet Lowell thought, as he smiled at the sheriff's amazement, that it merely emphasized the queer jumble of old and new on every reservation.

"I'll ask you to wait for me out there in the trees," said Fire Bear.

Redmond hesitated, but the agent turned at once and walked away, and the sheriff finally followed. Fire Bear exhorted his followers a few moments, and then disappeared in his tent. Soon he came out, dressed in the "store clothes" of the ordinary Indian. He joined Redmond and the agent at the edge of the glade, and they made their way toward the creek, no one venturing to follow from the camp. At the bottom of the slope they found the Indian helpers with the horses.

"Fire Bear," said Lowell, as they paused before starting out, "there's one thing more I want of you. Help us to find Jim McFann. He's as deep or deeper in this thing than you are."

"I know he is," replied Fire Bear, "but it wasn't for me to say so. I'll help find him for you."

They had to fight to get Jim McFann. They found the half-breed cooking some bacon over a tiny fire, at the head of a gulch that was just made for human concealment. If it had not been for the good offices of Fire Bear on the trail, they might have hunted a week for their man. McFann had moved camp several times since Plenty Buffalo had located him. Each time he had covered his tracks with surpassing care.

Lowell, according to prearranged plan, had walked in upon McFann, with Redmond covering the half-breed, ready to shoot in case a weapon was drawn. But McFann merely made a headlong dive for Lowell's legs, and there was a rough-and-tumble fight about the camp-fire which was settled only when the agent managed to get a lock on his wiry opponent which pinned McFann's back to the ground.

"You wouldn't fight that hard if you thought you was being yanked up for a little bootlegging, Jim," mused Tom Redmond, pulling his long mustache. "You know what we've come after you for, don't you?"

McFann threshed about in another futile attempt to escape, and cursed his captors with gifts of expletive which came from two races.

"It's on account of that tenderfoot that was found on the Dollar Sign," growled Jim, "but Fire Bear and his gang can't tell any more on me than I can on them."

"That's the way to get at the truth," chuckled the sheriff triumphantly. "I guess by the time you fellers are through with each other we'll know who shot that man and staked him down."

CHAPTER V

On the day following the incarceration of Fire Bear and Jim McFann, Lowell rode over to the scene of the murder on the Dollar Sign road.

It seemed to the agent as if a fresh start from the very beginning would do more than anything else to put him on the trail of a solution of the mystery.

Lowell was not inclined to accept Redmond's comfortable theory that either Fire Bear or Jim McFann was guilty—or that both were equally deep in the crime. Nor did he assume that these men were not guilty. It was merely that there were some aspects of the case which did not seem to him entirely convincing. Circumstantial evidence pointed strongly to Fire Bear and the half-breed, and this evidence might prove all that was necessary to fasten the crime upon the prisoners. In fact Redmond was so confident that he prophesied a confession from one or both of the men before the time arrived for their hearing in court.

As Lowell approached Talpers's store, the trader came out and hailed him.

"I hear Redmond's arrested Fire Bear and Jim McFann," said Talpers.

"Yes."

"Well, as far as public opinion goes, I s'pose Tom has hit the nail on the head," observed Bill. "There's some talk right now about lynchin' the prisoners. Folks wouldn't talk that way unless the arrest was pretty popular."

"That's Tom Redmond's lookout. He will have to guard against a lynching."

Talpers stroked his beard and smiled reflectively. Evidently he had something on his mind. His attitude was that of a man concealing something of the greatest importance.

"There's one thing sure," went on Bill. "Jim McFann ain't any more guilty of a hand in that murder than if he wasn't within a thousand miles of the Dollar Sign when the thing happened."

"That will have to be proved in court."

"Well, as far as McFann's concerned I know Redmond's barkin' up the wrong tree."

"How do you know it?"

Talpers made a deprecating motion.

"Of course I don't know it absolutely. It's jest what I feel, from bein' as well acquainted with Jim as I am."

"Yes, you and Jim are tolerably close to each other—everybody knows that."

Talpers shot a suspicious glance at the agent, and then he reassumed his mysterious grin.

"Where you goin' now?" he asked.

"Just up on the hill."

"I've been back there a couple of times," sneered Bill, "but I couldn't find no notes dropped by the murderer."

"Well, there's just one thing that's plain enough now, Talpers," said Lowell grimly, as he released his brakes. "While Jim McFann is in jail a lot of Indians are going to be thirsty, and your receipts for whiskey are not going to be so big."

Talpers scowled angrily and stepped toward the agent. Lowell sat calmly in the car, watching him unconcernedly. Then Talpers suddenly turned and walked toward the store, and the agent started his motor and glided away.

Bill's ugly scowl did not fade as he stalked into his store. Lowell's last shot about the bootlegging had gone home. Talpers had had more opposition from Lowell than from any other Indian agent since the trader had established his store on the reservation line. In fact the young agent had made whiskey-dealing so dangerous that Talpers was getting worried. Lowell had brought the Indian police to a state of efficiency never before obtained. Bootlegging had become correspondingly difficult. Jim McFann had complained several times about being too close to capture. Now he was arrested on another charge, and, as Lowell had said, Talpers's most profitable line of business was certain to suffer. As Bill walked back to his store he wondered how much Lowell actually knew, and how much had been shrewd guesswork. The young agent had a certain inscrutable air about him, for all his youth, which was most disturbing.

Talpers had not dared come out too openly for McFann's release. He offered bail bonds, which were refused. He had managed to get a few minutes' talk with McFann, but Redmond insisted on being present, and all the trader could do was to assure the half-breed that everything possible would be done to secure his release.

Bill's disturbed condition of mind vanished only when he reached into his pocket and drew out the letter which indicated that the girl at Mystery Ranch knew something about the tragedy which was setting not only the county but the whole State aflame. Here was a trump card which might be played in several different ways. The thing to do was to hold it, and to keep his counsel until the right time came. He thanked the good fortune that had put him in possession of the postmastership—an office which few men were shrewd enough to use to their own good advantage! Any common postmaster, who couldn't use his brains, would have let that letter go right through, but that wasn't Bill Talpers's way! He read the letter over again, slowly, as he had done a dozen times before. Written in a pretty hand it was—handwriting befitting a dum fine-lookin' girl like that! Bill's features softened into something resembling a smile. He put the letter back in his pocket, and his expression was almost beatific as he turned to wait on an Indian woman who had come in search of a new shawl.

Talpers's attitude, which had been at once cynical and mysterious, was the cause of some speculation on Lowell's part as the agent drove away from the trader's store. Something had happened to put so much of triumph in Talpers's face and speech, but Lowell was not able to figure out just what that something could be. He resolved to keep a closer eye than customary on the doings of the trader, but soon all thoughts of everything save those concerned directly with the murder were banished from his mind when he reached the scene of the tragedy.

Getting out of his automobile, Lowell went over the ground carefully. The grass and even some of the sage had been trampled down by the curious crowds that had flocked to the scene. An hour's careful search revealed nothing, and Lowell walked back to his car, shaking his head. Apparently the surroundings were more inscrutable than ever. The rolling hills were beginning to lose their green tint, under a hot sun, unrelieved by rain. The last rain of the season had fallen a day or so before the murder. Lowell remembered the little pools he had splashed through on the road, and the scattered "wallows" of mud that had remained on the prairie. Such places were now all dry and caked. A few meadow-larks were still singing, but even their notes would be silenced in the long, hot days that were to come. But the distant mountains, and the little stream in the bottom of the valley, looked cool and inviting. Ordinarily Lowell would have turned his machine toward the line of willows and tried an hour or so of fly-fishing, as there were plenty of trout in the stream, but to-day he kept on along the road over which he had taken Helen Ervin to her stepfather's ranch.

As Lowell drove up in front of Willis Morgan's ranch-house, he noticed a change for the better in the appearance of the place. Wong had been doing some work on the fence, but had discreetly vanished when Lowell came in sight. The yard had been cleared of rubbish and a thick growth of weeds had been cut down.

Lowell marveled that a Chinese should be doing such work as repairing a fence, and wondered if the girl had wrought all the changes about the place or if it had been done under Morgan's direction.

As if in answer, Helen Ervin came into the yard with a rake in her hand. She gave a little cry of pleasure at seeing Lowell.

"I'd have been over before, as I promised," said Lowell, "and in fact I had actually started when I had to make a long trip to a distant part of the reservation."

"I suppose it was in connection with this murder," she said.

"Yes."

"Tell me about it. What bearing did your trip have on it?"

Lowell was surprised at the intensity of her question.

"Well, you see," he said, "I had to bring in a couple of men who are suspected of committing the crime. But, frankly, I thought that in this quiet place you had not so much as heard of the murder."

The girl smiled, but there was no mirth in her eyes.

"Of course it isn't as if one had newsboys shouting at the door," she replied, "but we couldn't escape hearing of it, even here. Tell me, who are these men you have arrested?"

"An Indian and a half-breed. Their tracks were found at the scene of the murder."

"But that evidence is so slight! Surely they cannot—they may not be guilty."

"If not, they will have to clear themselves at the trial."

"Will they—will they be hanged if found guilty?"

"They may be lynched before the trial. There is talk of it now."

Helen made a despairing gesture.

"Don't let anything of that sort happen!" she cried. "Use all your influence. Get the men out of the country if you can. But don't let innocent men be slain."

Lowell attempted to divert her mind to other things. He spoke of the changed appearance of the ranch.

"Your coming has made a great difference here," he said. "This doesn't look like the place where I left you not many days ago."

Helen closed her eyes involuntarily, as if to blot out some vision in her memory.

"That terrible night!" she exclaimed. "I—"

She paused, and Lowell looked at her in surprise and alarm.

"What is it?" he asked. "Is there anything wrong—anything I can do to help you?"

"No," she said. "Truly there is not, now. But there was. It was only the recollection of my coming here that made me act so queerly."

"Look here," said Lowell bluntly, "is that stepfather of yours treating you all right? To put it frankly, he hasn't a very good reputation around here. I've often regretted not telling you more when I brought you over here. But you know how people feel about minding their own affairs. It's a foolish sort of reserve that keeps us quiet when we feel that we should speak."

"No, I'm treated all right," said the girl. "It was just homesickness for my school, I guess, that worked on me when I first came here. But I can't get over the recollection of that night you brought me to this place. Everything seemed so chilling and desolate—and dead! And then those few days that followed!"

She buried her face in her hands a moment, and then said, quietly:

"Did you know that my stepfather had married an Indian woman?"

"Yes. Do you mean that you didn't know?"

"No, I didn't know."

"What a fool I was for not telling you these things!" exclaimed Lowell. "I might have saved you a lot of humiliation."

"You could have saved me more than humiliation. He told me all about her—the Indian woman. He laughed when he told me. He said he was going to kill me as he had killed her—by inches."

Lowell grew cold with horror.

"But this is criminal!" he declared. "Let me take you away from this place at once. I'll find some place where you can go—back to my mother's home in the East."

"No, it's all right now. I'm in no danger, and I can't leave this place. In fact I don't want to," said the girl, putting her hand on Lowell's arm.

"Do you mean to tell me that he treated you so fiendishly during the first few days, and then suddenly changed and became the most considerate of relatives?"

"I tell you I am being treated all right now. I merely told you what happened at first—part of the cruel things he said—because I couldn't keep it all to myself any longer. Besides, that Indian woman—poor little thing!—is on my mind all the time."

"Then you won't come away?"

"No—he needs me."

"Well, this beats anything I ever heard of—" began Lowell. Then he stopped after a glance at her face. She was deathly pale. Her eyes were unnaturally bright, and her hands trembled. It seemed to him that the school-girl he had brought to the ranch a few days before had become a woman through some great mental trial.

"Come and see, or hear, for yourself," said Helen.

Wonderingly, Lowell stepped into the ranch-house kitchen. Helen pointed to the living-room.

Through the partly open door, Lowell caught a glimpse of an aristocratic face, surmounted by gray hair. A white hand drummed on the arm of a library chair which contained pillows and blankets. From the room there came a voice that brought to Lowell a sharp and disagreeable memory of the cutting voice he had heard in false welcome to Helen Ervin a few days before. Only now there was querulous insistence in the voice—the insistence of the sick person who calls upon some one who has proved unfailing in the performance of the tasks of the sick-room.

Helen stepped inside the room and closed the door. Lowell heard her talking soothingly to the sick man, and then she came out.

"You have seen for yourself," she said.

Lowell nodded, and they stepped out into the yard once more.

"I'll leave matters to your own judgment," said Lowell, "only I'm asking two things of you. One is to let me know if things go wrong, and the other isn't quite so important, but it will please me a lot. It's just to go riding with me right now."

Helen smilingly assented. Once more she was the girl he had brought over from the agency. She ran indoors and spoke a few words to Wong, and came out putting on her hat.

They drove for miles toward the heart of the Indian reservation. The road had changed to narrow, parallel ribbons, with grass between. Cattle, some of which belonged to the Indians and some to white leasers, were grazing in the distance. Occasionally they could see an Indian habitation—generally a log cabin, with its ugliness emphasized by the grace of a flanking tepee. Everything relating to human affairs seemed dwarfed in such immensity. The voices of Indian herdsmen, calling to each other, were reduced to faint murmurs. The very sound of the motor seemed blanketed.

Lowell and the girl traveled for miles in silence. He shrewdly suspected that the infinite peace of the landscape would prove the best tonic for her overwrought mind. His theory proved correct. The girl leaned back in the seat, and, taking off her hat, enjoyed to the utmost the rush of the breeze and the swift changes in the great panorama.

"It isn't any wonder that the Indians fought hard for this country, is it?" asked Lowell. "It's all too big for one's comprehension at first, especially when you've come from brick walls and mere strips of sky, but after you've become used to it you can never forget it."

"I'd like to keep right on going to those blue mountains," said the girl. "It's wonderful, but a bit appalling, to a tenderfoot such as I am. I think we'd better go back."

Lowell drove in a circuitous route instead of taking the back trail. Just after they had swung once more into the road near the ranch, they met a horseman who proved to be Bill Talpers. The trader reined his horse to the side of the road and motioned to Lowell to stop. Bill's grin was bestowed upon the girl, who uttered a little exclamation of dismay when she established the identity of the horseman.

"I jest wanted to ask if you found anything up there," said Bill, jerking his thumb toward the road over which he had just ridden. It was quite plain that Talpers had been drinking.

"Maybe I did, and maybe not, Bill," answered Lowell disgustedly. "Anyway, what about it?"

"Jest this," observed Bill, talking to Lowell, but keeping his gaze upon Helen. "Sometimes you can find letters where you don't expect the guilty parties to leave 'em. Mebbe you ain't lookin' in the right place for evidence. How-de-do, Miss Ervin? I'm goin' to drop in at the ranch and see you and your stepfather some day. I ain't been very neighborly so far, but it's because business has prevented."

Lowell started the car, and as they darted away he looked in astonishment at the girl. Her pallor showed that once more she was under great mental strain. It came to Lowell in a flash that Bill's arrogance sprang from something deeper than mere conceit or drunkenness. Undoubtedly he had set out deliberately to terrorize the girl, and had succeeded. Lowell waited for some remark from Helen, but none came. He kept back the questions that were on the tip of his tongue. Aside from a few banalities, they exchanged no words until Lowell helped her from the car at the ranch.

"I want to tell you," said Lowell, "that I appreciate such confidence as you have reposed in me. I won't urge you to tell more but I'm going to be around in the offing, and, if things don't go right, and especially if Bill Talpers—"

There was so much terror in the girl's eyes that Lowell's assurances came to a lame ending. She turned and ran into the house, after a fluttering word of thanks for the ride, and Lowell, more puzzled than ever, drove thoughtfully away.

CHAPTER VI

White Lodge was a town founded on excitement. Counting its numerous shootings and consequent lynchings, and proportioning them to its population, White Lodge had experienced more thrills than the largest of Eastern cities. Some ribald verse-writer, seizing upon White Lodge's weakness as a theme, had once written:

We can put the card deck by us,
We can give up whiskey straight;
Though we ain't exactly pious,
We can fill the parson's plate;
We can close the gamblin' places,
We can save our hard-earned coin,
BUT we want a man for breakfast
In the mor-r-rnin'.

But of course such lines were written in early days, and for newspaper consumption in a rival town. White Lodge had grown distinctly away from its wildness. It had formed a Chamber of Commerce which entered bravely upon its mission as a lodestone for the attraction of Eastern capital. But the lure of adventurous days still remained in the atmosphere. Men who were assembled for the purpose of seeing what could be done about getting a horseshoe-nail factory for White Lodge wound up the session by talking about the days of the cattle and sheep war. All of which was natural, and would have taken place in any town with White Lodge's background of stirring tradition.

Until the murder on the Dollar Sign road there had been little but tradition for White Lodge to feed on. The sheriff's job had come to be looked upon as a sinecure. But now all was changed. Not only White Lodge, but the whole countryside, had something live to discuss. Even old Ed Halsey, who had not been down from his cabin in the mountains for at least five years, ambled in on his ancient saddle horse to get the latest in mass theory.

So far as theorizing was concerned, opinion in White Lodge ran all one way. The men who had been arrested were guilty, so the local newspaper assumed, echoing side-walk conversation. The only questions were: Just how was the crime committed, and how deeply was each man implicated?

Also, were there any confederates? Some of the older cattlemen, who had been shut out of leases on the reservation, were even heard to hint that in their opinion the whole tribe might have had a hand in the killing. Anyway, Fire Bear's cohorts should be rounded up and imprisoned without delay.

Lowell was not surprised to find that he had been drawn into the vortex of unfriendliness. More articles and editorials appeared in the "White Lodge Weekly Star," putting the general blame for the tragedy upon the policy of "coddling" the Indians.

"The whole thing," wound up one editorial, "is the best kind of an argument for throwing open the reservation to white settlement."

"That is the heart of the matter as it stands," said Lowell, pointing out the editorial to his chief clerk. "This murder is to be made the excuse for a big drive on Congress to have the reservation thrown open."

"Yes," observed Rogers, "the big cattlemen have been itching for another chance since their last bill was defeated in Congress. They remind me of the detective concern that never sleeps, only they might better get in a few honest, healthy snores than waste their time the way they have lately."

Lowell paid no attention to editorial criticism, but it was not easy to avoid hearing some of the personal comment that was passed when he visited White Lodge. In fact he found it necessary to come to blows with one cowpuncher, who had evidently been stationed near Lowell's automobile to "get the goat" of the young Indian agent. The encounter had been short and decisive. The cowboy, who was the hero of many fistic engagements, passed some comment which had been elaborately thought out at the campfire, and which, it was figured by his collaborators, "would make anything human fight or quit."

"That big cowpuncher from Sartwell's outfit sure got the agent's goat all right," said Sheriff Tom Redmond, in front of whose office the affair happened. "That is to say, he got the goat coming head-on, horns down and hoofs striking fire. That young feller was under the cowpuncher's arms in jest one twenty-eighth of a second, and there was only two sounds that fell on the naked ear—one being the smack when Lowell hit and the other the crash when the cowpuncher lit. If that rash feller'd taken the trouble to send me a little note of inquiry in advance, I could have told him to steer clear of a man who tied into a desperate man the way that young agent tied into Jim McFann out there on the reservation. But no public or private warnings are going to be necessary now. From this time on, young Lowell's going to have more berth-room than a wildcat."

Such matters as cold nods from former friends were disregarded by Lowell. He had been through lesser affairs which had brought him under criticism. In fact he knew that a certain measure of such injustice would be the portion of any man who accepted the post of agent. He went his way, doing what he could to insure a fair trial for both men, and at the same time not overlooking anything that might shed new light on a case which most of the residents of White Lodge seemed to consider as closed, all but the punishment to be meted out to the prisoners.

The hearing was to be held in the little court-room presided over by Judge Garford, who had been a figure at Vigilante trials in early days and who was a unique personification of kindliness and firmness. Both prisoners had refused counsel, nor had any confession materialized, as Tom Redmond had prophesied. McFann had spent most of his time cursing all who had been concerned in his arrest. Talpers had called on him again, and had whispered mysteriously through the bars:

"Don't worry, Jim. If it comes to a showdown, I'll be there with evidence that'll clear you flyin'."

As a matter of fact, Talpers intended to play a double game. He would let matters drift, and see if McFann did not get off in the ordinary course of events. Meantime the trader would use his precious possession, the letter written by Helen Ervin, to terrify the girl. In case the girl proved defiant, why, then it would be time to produce the letter as a law-abiding citizen should, and demand that the searchlight of justice be turned on the author of a missive apparently so directly concerned with the murder. If it so happened that the letter in his hands proved to be a successful weapon, and if Bill Talpers were accepted as a suitor, he would let the matter drop, so far as the authorities were concerned—and Jim McFann could drop with it. If the half-breed were to be sacrificed when a few words from Bill Talpers might save him, so much the worse for Jim McFann! The affairs of Bill Talpers were to be considered first of all, and there was no need of being too solicitous over the welfare of any mere cat's-paw like the half-breed.

If Jim McFann had known what was passing in the mind of the trader, he would have torn his way out of jail with his bare hands and slain his partner in bootlegging. But the half-breed took Talpers's fair words at face value and faced his prospects with a trifle more of equanimity.

Fire Bear continued to view matters with true Indian composure. He had made no protestations of innocence, and had told Lowell there was nothing he wanted except to get the hearing over with as quickly as possible. The young Indian, to Lowell's shrewd eye, did not seem well. His actions were feverish and his eyes unnaturally bright. At Lowell's request, an agency doctor was brought and examined Fire Bear. His report to Lowell was the one sinister word: "Tuberculosis!"

When the men were brought into the court-room a miscellaneous crowd had assembled. Cowpunchers from many miles away had ridden in to hear what the Indian and "breed" had to say for themselves. The crowd even extended through the open doors into the hallway. Late comers, who could not get so much as standing room, draped themselves upon the stairs and about the porch and made eager inquiry as to the progress of affairs.

Helen Ervin rode in to attend the hearing, in response to an inner appeal against which she had struggled vainly. She met Lowell as she dismounted from the old white horse in front of the court-house. Lowell had called two or three times at the ranch, following their ride across the reservation. He had not gone into the house, but had merely stopped to get her assurance that everything was going well and that the sick man was steadily progressing toward convalescence.

"Why didn't you tell me you were coming over?" asked Lowell. "I would have brought you in my machine. As it is, I must insist on taking you back. I'll have Plenty Buffalo lead your pony back to the ranch when he returns to the agency."

"I couldn't help coming," said Helen. "I have a feeling that innocent men are going to suffer a great injustice. Tell me, do you think they have a chance of going free?"

"They may be held for trial," said Lowell. "No one knows what will be brought up either for or against them in the meantime."

"But they should not spend so much as a day in jail," insisted Helen. "They—"

Here she paused and looked over Lowell's shoulder, her expression changing to alarm. The agent turned and beheld Bill Talpers near them, his gaze fixed on the girl. Talpers turned away as Lowell escorted Helen upstairs to the court-room, where he secured a seat for her.

As the prisoners were brought in Helen recognized the unfriendliness of the general attitude of White Lodge toward them. Hostility was expressed in cold stares and whispered comment.

The men afforded a contrasting picture. Fire Bear's features were pure Indian. His nose was aquiline, his cheek-bones high, and his eyes black and piercing, the intensity of their gaze being emphasized by the fever which was beginning to consume him. His expression was martial. In his football days the "fighting face" of the Indian star had often appeared on sporting pages. He surveyed the crowd in the court-room with calm indifference, and seldom glanced at the gray-bearded, benign-looking judge.

Jim McFann, on the contrary, seldom took his eyes from the judge's face. Jim was not so tall as Fire Bear, but was of wiry, athletic build. His cheek-bones were as high as those of the Indian, but his skin was lighter in color, and his hair had a tendency to curl. His sinewy hands were clenched on his knees, and his moccasined feet crossed and uncrossed themselves as the hearing progressed.

Each man testified briefly in his own behalf, and each, in Helen's opinion, told a convincing story. Both admitted having been on the scene of the crime. Jim McFann was there first. The half-breed testified that he had been looking for a rawhide lariat which he thought he had dropped from his saddle somewhere along the Dollar Sign road the day before. He had noticed an automobile standing in the road, and had discovered the body staked down on the prairie. In answer to a question, McFann admitted that the rope which had been cut in short lengths and used to tie the murdered man to the stakes had been the lariat for which he had been searching. He was alarmed at this discovery, and was about to remove the rope from the victim's ankles and wrists, when he had descried a body of horsemen approaching. He had thought the horsemen might be Indian police, and had jumped on his horse and ridden away, making his way through a near-by gulch and out on the prairie without being detected.

"Why were you so afraid of the Indian police?" was asked.

The half-breed hesitated a moment, and then said:

"Bootlegging."

There was a laugh in the court-room at this—a sharp, mirthless laugh which was checked by the insistent sound of the bailiff's gavel.

Jim McFann sank back in his chair, livid with rage. In his eyes was the look of the snarling wild animal—the same look that had flashed there when he sprang at Lowell in his camp. He motioned that he had nothing more to say.

Fire Bear's testimony was as brief. He said that he and a company of his young men—perhaps thirty or forty—all mounted on ponies, had taken a long ride from the camp where they had been making medicine. The trip was in connection with the medicine that was being made. Fire Bear and his young men had ridden by a circuitous route, and had left the reservation at the Greek Letter Ranch on the same morning that McFann had found the slain man's body. They had intended riding along the Dollar Sign road, past Talpers's and the agency, and back to their camp. But on the big hill between Talpers's and the Greek Letter Ranch they had found the automobile standing in the road, and a few minutes later had found the body, just as McFann had described it. They had not seen any trace of McFann, but had noticed the tracks of a man and pony about the automobile and the body. The Indians had held a quick consultation, and, on the advice of Fire Bear, had quit the scene suddenly. It was the murder of a white man, off the reservation. It was a case for white men to settle. If the Indians were found there, they might get in trouble. They had galloped across the prairie to their camp, by the most direct way, and had not gone on to Talpers's nor to the agency.

Helen expected both men to be freed at once. To her dismay, the judge announced that both would be held for trial, without bail, following perfunctory statements from Plenty Buffalo, Walter Lowell, and Sheriff Tom Redmond, relating to later events in the tragedy. As in a dream Helen saw some of the spectators starting to leave and Redmond's deputy beckon to his prisoners, when Walter Lowell rose and asked permission to address the court in behalf of the Government's ward, Fire Bear.

Lowell, in a few words, explained that further imprisonment probably would be fatal to Fire Bear. He produced the certificate of the agency physician, showing that the prisoner had contracted tuberculosis.

"If Fire Bear will give me his word of honor that he will not try to escape," said the agent, "I will guarantee his appearance on the day set for his trial."

A murmur ran through the court-room, quickly hushed by the insistent gavel.

Lowell had been reasonably sure of his ground before he spoke. The venerable judge had always been interested in the work at the agency, and was a close student of Indian tradition and history. The request had come as a surprise, but the court hesitated only a moment, and then announced that, if the Government's agent on the reservation would be responsible for the delivery of the prisoner for trial, the defendant, Fire Bear, would be delivered to said agent's care. The other defendant, being in good health and not being a ward of the Government, would have to stand committed to jail for trial.

Fire Bear accepted the news with outward indifference. Jim McFann, with his hands tightly clenched and the big veins on his forehead testifying to the rage that burned within him, was led away between Redmond and his deputy. There was a shuffling of feet and clinking of spurs as men rose from their seats. A buzz came from the crowd, as distinctly hostile as a rattler's whirr. Words were not distinguishable, but the sentiment could not have been any more distinctly indicated if the crowd had shouted in unison.

Judge Garford rose and looked in a fatherly way upon the crowd. At a motion from him the bailiff rapped for attention. The judge stroked his white beard and said softly:

"Friends, there is some danger that excitement may run away with this community. The arm of the law is long, and I want to say that it will be reached out, without fear or favor, to gather in any who may attempt in any way to interfere with the administration of justice."

To Helen it seemed as if the old, heroic West had spoken through this fearless giant of other days. There was no mistaking the meaning that ran through that quietly worded message. It brought the crowd up with a thrill of apprehension, followed by honest shame. There was even a ripple of applause. The crowd started once more to file out, but in different mood. Some of the more impetuous, who had rushed downstairs before the judge had spoken, were hustled away from the agent's automobile, around which they had grouped themselves threateningly.

"The judge means business," one old-timer said in an awe-stricken voice. "That's the way he looked and talked when he headed the Vigilantes' court. He'll do what he says if he has to hang a dozen men."

When Lowell and Helen came out to the automobile, followed by Fire Bear, the court-house square was almost deserted. Fire Bear climbed into the back seat, at Lowell's direction. He was without manacles. Helen occupied the seat beside the driver. As they drove away, she caught a glimpse of Judge Garford coming down the court-house steps. He was engaged in telling some bit of pioneer reminiscence—something broadly pleasant. His face was smiling and his blue eyes were twinkling. He looked almost as any grandparent might have looked going to join a favorite grandchild at a park bench. Yet here was a man who had torn aside the veil and permitted one glimpse at the old, inspiring West.

Helen turned and looked at him again, as, in an earlier era, she would have looked at Lincoln.

CHAPTER VII

The stage station at White Lodge was a temporary center of public interest every afternoon at three o'clock when Charley Hicks drove the passenger bus in from Quaking-Asp Grove. After a due inspection of the passengers the crowd always shifted immediately to the post-office to await the distribution of mail.

A well-dressed, refined-looking woman of middle age was among the passengers on the second day after the hearing of Fire Bear and Jim McFann. She had little or nothing to say on the trip—perhaps for the reason that speech would have been difficult on account of the monopolizing of the conversation by the other passengers. These included two women from White Lodge, one rancher from Antelope Mesa, and two drummers who were going to call on White Lodge merchants. The conversation was unusually brisk and ran almost exclusively on the murder.

Judge Garford's action in releasing Fire Bear on the agent's promise to produce the prisoner in court was the cause of considerable criticism. The two women, the ranchman, and one of the drummers had voted that too much leniency was shown. The other drummer appealed to the stage-driver to support his contention that the court's action was novel, but entirely just.

"Well, all I can say is," remarked the driver, "that if that Injun shows up for trial, as per his agreement, without havin' to be sent for, it's goin' to be a hard lesson for the white race to swaller. You can imagine how much court'd be held if all white suspects was to be let go on their word that they'd show up for trial. Detectives 'd be chasin' fugitives all over the universe. If that Injun shows up, I'll carry the hull reservation anywheres, without tickets, if they'll promise to pay me at the end of the trip."

The driver noticed that the quiet lady in the back seat, though taking no part in the conversation, seemed to be a keenly interested listener. No part of the discussion of the murder escaped her, but she asked no questions. On alighting at White Lodge, she asked the driver where she could get a conveyance to take her to Willis Morgan's ranch.

The driver looked at her in such astonishment that she repeated her question.

"I'd 'a' plum forgot there was such a man in this part of the country," said Charley, "if it hadn't 'a' been that sometime before this here murder I carried a young woman—a stepdaughter of his'n—and she asked me the same question. I don't believe you can hire any one to take you out there, but I'll bet I can get you took by the same young feller that took this girl to the ranch. He's the Indian agent, and I seen him in his car when we turned this last corner."

Followed by his passenger the driver hurried back to the corner and hailed Walter Lowell, who was just preparing to return to the agency.

On having matters explained, Lowell expressed his willingness to carry the lady passenger over to the ranch. Her suitcase was put in the automobile, and soon they were on the outskirts of White Lodge.

"I ought to explain," said the agent's passenger, "that my name is Scovill—Miss Sarah Scovill—and Mr. Morgan's stepdaughter has been in my school for years."

"I know," said Lowell. "I've heard her talk about your school, and I'm glad you're going out to see her. She needs you."

Miss Scovill looked quickly at Lowell. She was one of those women whose beauty is only accentuated by gray hair. Her brow and eyes were serene—those of a dreamer. Her mouth and chin were delicately modeled, but firm. Their firmness explained, perhaps, why she was executive head of a school instead of merely a teacher. Not all her philosophy had been won from books. She had traveled and observed much of life at first hand. That was why she could keep her counsel—why she had kept it during all the talk on the stage, even though that talk had vitally interested her. She showed the effects of her long, hard trip, but would not hear of stopping at the agency for supper.

"If you don't mind—if it is not altogether too much trouble to put you to—I must go on," she said. "I assure you it's very important, and it concerns Helen Ervin, and I assume that you are her friend."

Lowell hastened his pace. It all meant that it would be long past the supper hour when he returned to the agency, but there was an appeal in Miss Scovill's eyes and voice which was not to be resisted. Anyway, he was not going to offer material resistance to something which was concerned with the well being of Helen Ervin.

They sped through the agency, past Talpers's store, and climbed the big hill just as the purples fell into their accustomed places in the hollows of the plain. As they bowled past the scene of the tragedy, Lowell pointed it out, with only a brief word. His passenger gave a little gasp of pain and horror. He thought it was nothing more than might ordinarily be expected under such circumstances, but, on looking at Miss Scovill, he was surprised to see her leaning back against the seat, almost fainting.

"By George!" said Lowell contritely, "I shouldn't have mentioned it to you."

He slowed down the car, but Miss Scovill sat upright and recovered her mental poise, though with evident effort.

"I'm glad you did mention it," she said, looking back as if fascinated. "Only, you see, I'd been hearing about the murder most of the day in the stage, and then this place is so big and wide and lonely! Please don't think I'm foolish."

"It's all because you're from the city and haven't proportioned things as yet," said Lowell. "Now all this loneliness seems kindly, to me. It's only crowds that seem cruel. I often envy trappers dying alone in such places. Also I can understand why the Indians wanted nothing better in death than to have their bodies hoisted high atop of a hill, with nothing to disturb."

As they rounded the top of the hill and the road came up behind them like an inverted curtain, Miss Scovill gave one last backward look. Lowell saw that she was weeping quietly, but unrestrainedly. He drove on in silence until he pulled the automobile up in front of the Morgan ranch.

"You'll find Miss Ervin here," said Lowell, stepping out of the car. "This is the Greek Letter Ranch."

If the prospect brought any new shock to Miss Scovill, she gave no indication of the fact. She answered Lowell steadily enough when he asked her when he should call for her on her return trip.

"My return trip will be right now," she said. "I've thought it all out—just what I'm to do, with your help. Please don't take my suitcase from the car. Just turn the car around, and be ready to take us back to-night—I mean Helen and myself. I intend to bring her right out and take her away from this place."

Wonderingly Lowell turned the car as she directed. Miss Scovill knocked at the ranch-house door. It was opened by Wong, and Miss Scovill stepped inside. The door closed again. Lowell rolled a cigarette and smoked it, and then rolled another. He was about to step out of the car and knock at the ranch-house door when Helen and Miss Scovill came out, each with an arm about the other's waist.

Miss Scovill's face looked whiter than ever in the moonlight.

"Something has happened," she said—"something that makes it impossible for me to go back—for Helen to go back with me to-night. If you can come and get me in the morning, I'll go back alone."

Lowell's amazement knew no bounds. Miss Scovill had made this long journey from San Francisco to get Helen—evidently to wrest her at once away from this ranch of mystery—and now she was going back alone, leaving the girl among the very influences she had intended to combat.

"Please, Mr. Lowell, do as she says," interposed Helen, whose demeanor was grave, but whose joy at this meeting with her teacher and foster mother shone in her eyes.

"Yes, yes—you'll have our thanks all through your life if you will take me back to-morrow and say nothing of what you have seen or heard," said Miss Scovill.

Lowell handed Miss Scovill's suitcase to the silent Wong, who had slipped out behind the women.

"I'm only too glad to be of service to you in any way," he said. "I'll be here in the morning early enough so you can catch the stage out of White Lodge."

Much smoking on the way home did not clear up the mystery for Lowell. Nor did sitting up and weighing the matter long after his usual bedtime bring him any nearer to answering the questions: Why did Miss Scovill come here determined to take Helen Ervin back to San Francisco with her? Why did Miss Scovill change her mind so completely after arriving at Morgan's ranch? Also why did said Miss Scovill betray such unusual agitation on passing the scene of the murder on the Dollar Sign road—a murder that she had been hearing discussed from all angles during the day?

This last question was intensified the next morning, when, with Helen in the back seat with Miss Scovill, Lowell drove back to White Lodge. When they passed the scene of the murder, Lowell took pains to notice that Miss Scovill betrayed no signs of mental strain. Yet only a few hours before she had been completely unnerved at passing by this same spot.

The women talked little on the trip to White Lodge. What talk there was between them was on school matters—mostly reminiscences of Helen's school-days. Lowell could not help thinking that they feared to talk of present matters—that something was weighing them down and crushing them into silence. But they parted calmly enough at White Lodge. After the stage had gone with Miss Scovill, Helen slipped into the seat beside Lowell and chatted somewhat as she had done during their first journey over the road.

As for Lowell, he dismissed for the moment all thoughts of tragedy and mystery from his mind, and gave himself up to the enjoyment of the ride. They stopped at the agency, and Helen called on some of the friends she had made on her first journey through. Lowell showed her about the grounds, and she took keen interest in all that had been done to improve the condition of the Indians.

"Of course the main object is to induce the Indian to work," said Lowell. "The agency is simply an experimental plant to show him the right methods. It was hard for the white man to leave the comfortable life of the savage and take up work. The trouble is that we're expecting the Indian to acquire in a generation the very things it took us ages to accept. That's why I haven't been in too great a hurry to shut down on dances and religious ceremonies. The Indian has had to assimilate too much, as it is. It seems to me that if he makes progress slowly that is about all that can be expected of him."

"It seems to me that saving the Indian from extermination, as all this work is helping to do, is among the greatest things in the world," said Helen. "The sad thing to me is that these people seem so remote from all help. The world forgets so easily what it can't see."

"Yes, there are no newspapers out here to get up Christmas charity drives, and there are few volunteer settlement workers to be called on for help at any time. And there are no charity balls for the Indian. It isn't that he wants charity so much as understanding."

"Understanding often comes quickest through charity," interposed Helen. "It seems to me that no one could ask a better life-work than to help these people."

"There's more to them than the world has been willing to concede," declared Lowell. "I never have subscribed to Parkman's theory that the Indian's mind moves in a beaten track and that his soul is dormant. The more I work among them the more respect I have for their capabilities."

Further talk of Indian affairs consumed the remainder of the trip. Lowell was an enthusiast in his work, though he seldom talked of it, preferring to let results speak for themselves. But he had found a ready and sympathetic listener. Furthermore, he wished to take the girl's mind from the matters that evidently were proving such a weight. He succeeded so well that not until they reached the ranch did her troubled expression return.

"Tell me," said Lowell, as he helped her from the automobile, "is he—is Morgan better, and is he treating you all right?"

"Yes, to both questions," said she. Then, after a moment's hesitation, she added: "Come in. Perhaps it will be possible for you to see him."

Lowell stepped into the room that served as Morgan's study. One wall was lined with books, Greek predominating. Helen knocked at the door of the adjoining room, and there came the clear, sharp, cynical voice that had aroused all the antagonism in Lowell's nature on his first visit.

"Come in, come in!" called the voice, as cold as ice crystals.

Helen entered, and closed the door. The voice could be heard, in different modulations, but always with profound cynicism as its basis.

Lowell, with a gesture of rage, stepped to the library table. He picked up a volume of Shakespeare's tragedies, and noticed that all references to killing and to bloodshed in general had been blotted out. Passage after passage was blackened with heavy lines in lead pencil. In astonishment, Lowell picked up another volume and found that the same thing had been done. Then the door opened and he heard the cutting voice say:

"Tell the interesting young agent that I am indisposed. I have never had a social caller within my doors here, and I do not wish to start now."

Helen came out and closed the door.

"You heard?" she asked.

"Yes," replied Lowell. "It's all right. I'm only sorry if my coming has caused you any additional pain or embarrassment. I won't ask you again what keeps you in an atmosphere like this, but any time you want to leave, command me on the instant."

"Please don't get our talk back where it was before," pleaded Helen, as they stepped out on the porch and Lowell said good-bye. "I've enjoyed the ride and the talk to-day because it all took me away from myself and from this place of horrors. But I can't leave here permanently, no matter how much I might desire it."

"It's all going to be just as you say," Lowell replied. "Some day I'll see through it all, perhaps, but right now I'm not trying very hard, because some way I feel that you don't want me to."

She shook hands with him gratefully, and Lowell drove slowly back to the agency, not forgetting his customary stop at the scene of the murder—a stop that proved fruitless as usual.

When he entered the agency office, Lowell was greeted with an excited hail from Ed Rogers.

"Here's news!" exclaimed the chief clerk. "Tom Redmond has telephoned over that Jim McFann has broken jail."

"How did he get away?"

"Jim had been hearing all this talk about lynching. It had been coming to him, bit by bit, in the jail, probably passed on by the other prisoners, and it got him all worked up. It seems that the jailer's kid, a boy about sixteen years old, had been in the habit of bringing Jim's meals. Also the kid had a habit of carrying Dad's keys around, just to show off. Instead of grabbing his soup, Jim grabbed the kid by the throat. Then he made the boy unlock the cell door and Jim slipped out, gagged the kid, and walked out of the jail. He jumped on a cowboy's pony in front of the jail, and was gone half an hour before the kid, who had been locked in Jim's cell, managed to attract attention. Tom Redmond wants you to get out the Indian police, because he's satisfied Jim has skipped to the reservation and is hiding somewhere in the hills."

CHAPTER VIII

"That there girl down at the Greek Letter Ranch is the best-lookin' girl in these parts. I was goin' to slick up and drop around to see her, but this here Injun agent got in ahead of me. A man with nothin' but a cowpony don't stand a show against a feller with an auto when it comes to callin' on girls these days."

The nasal, drawling voice of Andy Wolters, cowpuncher for one of the big leasing outfits on the Indian reservation, came to the ears of Bill Talpers as the trader sat behind his post-office box screen, scowling out upon a sunshiny world.

A chorus of laughter from other cowpunchers greeted the frank declaration of Mr. Wolters.

"Agent or no agent, you wouldn't stand a show with that girl," chimed in one of the punchers. "The squaw professor'd run you through the barb-wire fence so fast that you'd leave hide and clothes stickin' to it. Willis Morgan ain't ever had a visitor on his place sence he run the Greek Letter brand on his first steer."

"Well, he ain't got any more steers left. That old white horse is all the stock I see of his—anyways, it's all that's carryin' that pitchfork brand."

"You know what they say about how old Morgan got that pitchfork brand, don't you?—how he was huntin' through the brand book one night, turnin' the pages over and cussin' because nothin' seemed to suit his fancy, when all of a sudden there was a bright light and a strong smell of sulphur, and the devil himself was right there at Morgan's side. 'Use this for a brand,' says the devil, and there was the mark of his pitchfork burnt on Morgan's front door, right where you'll see it to-day if you ever want to go clost enough."

"Anyway, git that out of your head about Morgan's ranch never havin' any visitors," said another cowboy. "This here Injun agent's auto runs down there reg'lar. Must be that he's a kind of a Trilby and has got old Morgan hypnotized."

"Aw, you mean a Svengali."

"I bet you these spurs against a package of smokin' tobacco I know what I mean," stoutly asserted the cowpuncher whose literary knowledge had been called in question, and then the talk ran along the familiar argumentative channels that had no interest for Bill Talpers.

The trader looked back into the shadowy depths of his store. Besides the cowboys there were several Indians leaning against the counters or sitting lazily on boxes and barrels. Shelves and counters were piled with a colorful miscellany of goods calculated to appeal to primitive tastes. There were bright blankets and shawls, the latter greedily eyed by every Indian woman who came into the store. There were farming implements and boots and groceries and harness. In the corner where Bill Talpers sat was the most interesting collection of all. This corner was called the pawnshop. Here Bill paid cash for silver rings and bracelets, and for turquoise and other semi-precious stones either mounted or in the rough. Here he dickered for finely beaded moccasins and hat-bands and other articles for which he found a profitable market in the East. Here watches were put up for redemption, disappearing after they had hung their allotted time.

Traders on the reservation were not permitted to have such corners in their stores, but Bill, being over the line, drove such bargains as he pleased and took such security as he wished.

As Bill looked over his oft-appraised stock, it seemed to have lost much of its one-time charm. Storekeeping for a bunch of Indians and cowpunchers was no business for a smart, self-respecting man to be in—a man who had ambitions to be somebody in a busier world. The thing to do was to sell out and clear out—after he had married that girl at Morgan's ranch. He had been too lenient with that girl, anyway. Here he held the whip-hand over her and had never used it. He had been waiting from day to day, gloating over his opportunities, and this Indian agent had been calling on her and maybe was getting her confidence.

Maybe it had gone so far that the girl had told Lowell about the letter she had mailed and that Bill had held up. Something akin to a chill moved along Bill's spinal column at the thought. But of course such a thing could not be. The girl couldn't afford to talk about anything like that letter, which was certain to drag her into the murder.

Bill looked at the letter again and then tucked it back in the safe. That was the best place to keep it. It might get lost out of his pocket and then there'd be the very devil to pay. He knew it all by heart, anyway. It was enough to give him what he wanted—this girl for a wife. She simply couldn't resist, with that letter held over her by a determined man like Bill Talpers. After he had married her, he'd sell out this pile of junk and let somebody else haggle with the Injuns and cowpunchers. Bill Talpers'd go where he could wear good clothes every day, and his purty wife'd hold up her head with the best of them! He'd go over and state his case that very night. He'd lay down the law right, so this girl at Morgan's 'd know who her next boss was going to be. If Willis Morgan tried to interfere, Bill Talpers 'd crush him just the way he'd crushed many a rattler!

As a preliminary to his courting trip, Bill took a drink from a bottle that he kept handy in his corner. Then he walked out to his sleeping-quarters in the rear of the store and "slicked up a bit," during which process he took several drinks from another bottle which was stowed conveniently there.

Leaving his store in charge of his clerk, Bill rode over the Dollar Sign highway toward Morgan's ranch. The trader was dressed in black. A white shirt and white collar fairly hurt the eye, being in such sharp contrast with Bill's dark skin and darker beard. A black hat, wide of brim and carefully creased, replaced the nondescript felt affair which Bill usually wore. He donned the best pair of new boots that he could select from his stock. They hurt his feet so that he swung first one and then the other from the stirrups to get relief. There was none to tell Bill that his broad, powerful frame looked better in its everyday habiliments, and he would not have believed, even if he had been told. He had created a sensation as he had creaked through the store after his dressing-up operations had been completed, and he intended to repeat the thrill when he burst upon the vision of the girl at Morgan's.

Wong had cleared away the supper dishes at the Greek Letter Ranch, and had silently taken his way to the little bunkhouse which formed his sleeping-quarters.

In the library a lamp glowed. A gray-haired man sat at the table, bowed in thought. A girl, sitting across from him, was writing. Outside was the silence of the prairie night, broken by an occasional bird call near by.

"It is all so lonely here, I wonder how you can stand it," said the man. There was deep concern in his voice. All sharpness had gone from it.

"It is all different, of course, from the country in which I have been living, and it *is* lonely, but I could get used to it soon if it were not for this pall—"

Here the girl rose and went to the open window. She leaned on the sill and looked out.

The man's gaze followed her. She was even more attractive than usual, in a house dress of light color, her arms bare to the elbows, and her pale, expressive face limned against the black background of the night.

"I know what you would say," replied the man. "It would be bearable here—in fact, it might be enjoyable were it not for the black shadow upon us. Rather it is a shadow which is blood-red instead of black."

His voice rose, and excitement glowed in his deep-set, clear gray eyes. His face lost its pallor, and his well-shaped, yet strong hands clutched nervously at the arms of his chair.

The girl turned toward him soothingly, when both paused and listened.

"It is some Indian going by," said the man, as hoof-beats became distinct.

"The Indians don't ride this late. Besides, no Indian would stop here."

The man stepped to an adjoining room. As he disappeared, there came the sound of footfalls on the porch and Bill Talpers's heavy knock made the front door panels shake.

The girl hesitated a moment, and then opened the door. The trader walked in without invitation, his new boots squeaking noisily. If he had expected any exhibition of fear on the part of the girl, Talpers was mistaken. She looked at him calmly, and Bill shifted uneasily from one foot to another as he took off his hat.

"I thought I'd drop in for a little social call, seein' as you ain't called on me sence our talk about that letter," said Bill, seating himself at the table.

"It was what I might have expected," replied the girl.

"That's fine," said Bill amiably. "I'm tickled to know that you expected me."

"Yes, knowing what a coward you are, I thought you would come."

Talpers flushed angrily, and then grinned, until his alkali-cracked lips glistened in the lamplight.

"That's the spirit!" he exclaimed. "I never seen a more spunky woman, and that's the kind I like. But there ain't many humans that can call me a coward. I guess you don't know how many notches I've got on the handle of this forty-five, do you?" he asked, touching the gun that swung in a holster at his hip under his coat. "Well, there's three notches on there, and that don't count an Injun I got in a fair fight. I don't count any *coups* unless they're on white folks."

"I'm not interested in your record of bloodshed." The girl's voice was low, but it stung Bill to anger.

"Yes, you are," he retorted. "You're goin' to be mighty proud of your husband's record. You'll be glad to be known as the wife of Bill Talpers, who never backed down from no man. That's what I come over here for, to have you say that you'll marry me. If you don't say it, I'll have to give that letter over to the authorities at White Lodge. It sure would be a reg'lar bombshell in the case right now."

The trader's squat figure, in his black suit, against the white background made by the lamp, made the girl think of a huge, grotesque blot of ink. His broad, hairy hand rested on the table. She noticed the strong, thick fingers, devoid of flexibility, yet evidently of terrific strength.

"Now you and me," went on Talpers, "could get quietly married, and I could sell this store of mine for a good figger, and I'd be willin' to move anywheres you want—San Francisco, or Los Angeles, or San Diego, or anywheres. And I could burn up that letter, and there needn't nobody know that the wife of Bill Talpers was mixed up in the murder that is turnin' this here State upside down. Furthermore, jest to show you that Bill Talpers is a square sort, I won't ever ask you myself jest how deep and how wide you're in this murder, nor why you wrote that letter, nor what it was all about. Ain't that fair enough?"

The girl laughed.

"It's too fair," she said. "I can't believe you'd hold to such a bargain."

"You try me and see," urged Bill. "All you've got to do is to say you'll marry me."

"Well, I'll never say it."

"Yes, you will," huskily declared Bill, putting his hat on the table. "You'll say it right here, to-night. Your stepfather's sick, I hear. If he was feelin' his best he wouldn't be more'n a feather in my way—not more'n that Chinaman of yours. I've got to have your word to-night, or, by cripes, that letter goes to White Lodge!"

The girl was alarmed. She was colorless as marble, but her eyes were defiant. Talpers advanced toward her threateningly, and she retreated toward the door which opened into the other room. Bill swung her aside and placed himself squarely in front of the door, his arms outspread.

"No hide and seek goes," he said. "You stay in this room till you give me the right answer."

The girl ran toward the door opening into the kitchen. Talpers ran after her, clumsily but swiftly. The girl saw that she was going to be overtaken before reaching the door, and dodged to one side. The trader missed his grasp for her, and pitched forward, the force of his fall shaking the cabin. He struck his head against a corner of the table, and lay unconscious, spread out in a broad helplessness that made the girl think once more of spilled ink.

The white-haired man stood in the doorway to the other room. He held a revolver, with which he covered Talpers, but the trader did not move. The white-haired man deftly removed Talpers's revolver from its holster and put it on the table. Then he searched the trader's pockets.

"I'm glad I didn't have to shoot this swine," he said to the girl. "Another second and it would have been necessary. The letter isn't here, but you can frighten him with these trinkets—his own revolver and this watch which evidently he took from the murdered man on the hill. You know what else of Edward Sargent's belongings were taken."

The girl nodded.

"He will recover soon," went on the gray-haired man. "You will be in no further danger. He will be glad to go when he sees what evidence you have against him."

The white-haired man had taken a watch from one of Talpers's pockets. He put the timepiece on the table beside the trader's revolver. Then the door to the adjoining room closed again, and the girl was alone with the trader waiting for him to recover consciousness.

Soon Bill Talpers sat up. His hand went to his head and came away covered with blood. The world was rocking, and the girl at the table looked like half a dozen shapes in one.

"This is your own revolver pointed at you, Mr. Talpers," she said, "but this watch on the table, by which you will leave this house in three minutes, is not yours. It belonged once to Edward B. Sargent, and you are the man who took it."

Talpers tried to answer, but could not at once.

"You not only took this watch," said the girl slowly, "but you took money from that murdered man."

"It's all a lie," growled Bill at last.

"Wait till you hear the details. You took twenty-eight hundred dollars in large bills, and three hundred dollars in smaller bills."

Talpers looked at the girl in mingled terror and amazement. Guilt was in his face, and his fears made him forget his aching head.

"You kept this money and did not let your half-breed partner in crime know you had found it," went on the girl. "Also you kept the watch, and, as it had no mark of identification, you concluded you could safely wear it."

Talpers struggled dizzily to his feet.

"It's all lies," he repeated. "I didn't kill that man."

"You might find it hard to convince a jury that you did not, with such evidence against you."

The trader looked at the watch as if he intended to make a dash to recover it, but the girl kept him steadily covered with his own revolver. Muttering curses, and swaying uncertainly on his feet, Talpers seized his hat and rushed from the house. He could be heard fumbling with the reins at the gate, and then the sound of hoofs came in diminuendo as he rode away.

CHAPTER IX

In his capacity of Indian agent Walter Lowell often had occasion to scan the business deals of his more progressive wards. He was at once banker and confidant of most of the Indians who were getting ahead in agriculture and stock-raising. He did not seek such a position, nor did he discourage it. Though it cost him much extra time and work, he advised the Indians whenever requested.

One of the reservation's most prosperous stock-raisers, who had been given permission to sell off some of his cattle, came to Lowell with a thousand-dollar bill, asking if it were genuine.

"It's all right," said Lowell, "but where did you get it?"

The Indian said he had received it from Bill Talpers in the sale of some livestock. Lowell handed it back without comment, but soon afterward found occasion to call on Bill Talpers at the trader's store.

Bill had been a frequent and impartial visitor to the bottles that were tucked away at both ends of his store. His hands and voice were shaky. His hat was perched well forward on his head, covering a patch of court-plaster which his clerk had put over a scalp wound, following a painful process of hair-cutting. Bill had just been through the process of "bouncing" Andy Wolters, who remained outside, expressing wonder and indignation to all who called.

"All I did was ask Bill where his favorite gun was gone," quoth Andy in his nasal voice, as Lowell drove up to the store platform. "I never seen Bill without that gun before in my life. I jest started to kid him a little by askin' him who took it away from him, when he fired up and throwed me out of the store."

Lowell stepped inside the store.

"Bill," said Lowell, as the trader rose from his chair behind the screen of letter-boxes, "I want you to help me out in an important matter."

Bill's surprise showed in his swollen face.

"It's this," went on Lowell. "If any of the Indians bring anything here to pawn outside of the usual run of turquoise jewelry and spurs, I want you to let me know. Also, if they offer any big bills in payment for goods—say anything like a thousand-dollar bill—just give me the high sign, will you? It may afford a clue in this murder case."

Talpers darted a look of suspicion at the agent. Lowell's face was serene. He was leaning confidentially across the counter, and his eyes met Bill's in a look that made the trader turn away.

"You know," said Lowell, "it's quite possible that money and valuables were taken from Sargent's body. To be sure, they found his checkbook and papers, but they wouldn't be of use to anyone else. A man of Sargent's wealth must have had considerable ready cash with him, and yet none was found. He would hardly be likely to start out on a long trip across country without a watch, and yet nothing of the sort was discovered. That's why I thought that if any Indians came in here with large amounts of money, or if they tried to pawn valuables which might have belonged to a man in Sargent's position, you could help clear up matters."

Hatred and suspicion were mingled in Talpers's look. The trader had spent most of his hours, since his return from Morgan's ranch, cursing the folly that had led him into wearing Sargent's watch. And now came this young Indian agent, with talk about thousand-dollar bills. There was another mistake Bill had made. He should have taken those bills far away and had them exchanged for money of smaller denomination. But he had been hard-pressed for cash, and suspicion seemed to point in such convincing fashion toward Fire Bear and the other Indians that it did not seem possible that it could be shifted elsewhere. Yet all his confidence had been shaken when Helen Ervin had calmly and correctly recounted to him the exact things that he had taken from that body on the hill. Probably she had been talking to the agent and had told him all she knew.

"I know what you're drivin' at," snarled Bill, his rage getting the better of his judgment. "You've been talkin' to that girl at Morgan's ranch, and she's been tellin' you all she thinks she knows. But she'd better go slow with all her talk about valuables and thousand-dollar bills. She forgets that she's as deep in this thing as anybody and I've got the document to prove it."

The surprise in the Indian agent's face was too genuine to be mistaken. Talpers realized that he had been betrayed into overshooting his mark. The agent had been engaged in a little game of bluff, and Talpers had fallen into his trap.

"All this is mighty interesting to me, Bill," said Lowell, regaining his composure. "I just dropped in here, hoping for a little general cooperation on your part, and here I find that you know a lot more than anybody imagined."

"You ain't got anything on me," growled Bill, "and if you go spillin' any remarks around here, it's your death-warrant sure."

Lowell did not take his elbow from the counter. His leaning position brought out the breadth of his shoulders and emphasized the athletic lines of his figure. He did not seem ruffled at Bill's open threat. He regarded Talpers with a steady look which increased Bill's rage and fear.

"The trouble with you is that you're so dead set on protectin' them Injuns of yours," said the trader, "that you're around tryin' to throw suspicion on innocent white folks. The hull county knows that Fire Bear done that murder, and if you hadn't got him on to the reservation the jail'd been busted into and he'd been lynched as he ought to have been."

Bill waited for an answer, but none came. The young agent's steady, thoughtful scrutiny was not broken.

"You've coddled them Injuns ever sence you've been on the job," went on Bill, casting aside discretion, "and now you're encouragin' them in downright murder. Here this young cuss, Fire Bear, is traipsin' around as he pleases, on nothin' more than his word that he'll appear for trial. But when Jim McFann busts out of jail, you rush out the hull Injun police force to run him down. And now here you are around, off the reservation, tryin' to saddle suspicion on your betters. It ain't right, I claim. Self-respectin' white men ought to have more protection around here."

Talpers's voice had taken on something of a whine, and Lowell straightened up in disgust.

"Bill," he said, "you aren't as much of a man as I gave you credit for being, and what's more you've been in some crooked game, just as sure as thousand-dollar bills have four figures on them."

Paying no attention to the imprecations which Talpers hurled after him, the agent went back to his automobile and turned toward the agency. He had intended going on to the Greek Letter Ranch, but Talpers's words had caused him to make a change in his plans. At the agency he brought out a saddle horse, and, following a trail across the undulating hills on the reservation, reached the wagon-road below the ranch, without arousing Talpers's suspicion.

As he tied his pony at the gate, Lowell noticed further improvement in the general appearance of the ranch.

"Somebody more than Wong has been doing this heavy work," he said to Helen, who had come out to greet him. "It must be that Morgan—your stepfather is well enough to help. Anyway, the ranch looks better every time I come."

"Yes, he is helping some," said Helen uneasily. "But I'm getting to be a first-rate ranch-woman. I had no idea it was so much fun running a place like this."

"I came over to see if you couldn't take time enough off for a little horseback ride," said Lowell. "This is a country for the saddle, after all. I still get more enjoyment from a good horseback ride than from a dozen automobile trips. I'll saddle up the old white horse while you get ready."

Helen ran indoors, and Lowell went to the barn and proceeded to saddle the white horse that bore the Greek Letter brand. The smiling Wong came out to cast an approving eye over the work.

"This old fly-fighter's a pretty good horse for one of his age, isn't he, Wong?" said Lowell, giving a last shake to the saddle, after the cinch had been tightened.

In shattered English Wong went into ecstasies over the white horse. Then he said, suddenly and mysteriously:

"You know Talpels?"

"You mean Bill Talpers?" asked Lowell. "What about him?"

Once more the dominant tongue of the Occident staggered beneath Wong's assault, as the cook described, partly in pantomime, the manner of Bill Talpers's downfall the night before.

"Do you mean to say that Talpers was over here last night and that here is where he got that scalp-wound?" demanded Lowell.

Wong grinned assent, and then vanished, after making a sign calling for secrecy on Lowell's part, as Helen arrived, ready for the ride.

Lowell was a good horseman, and the saddle had become Helen's chief means of recreation. In fact riding seemed to bring to her the only contentment she had known since she had come to the Greek Letter Ranch. She had overcome her first fear of the Indians. All her rides that were taken alone were toward the reservation, as she had studiously avoided going near Talpers's place. Also she did not like to ride past the hill on the Dollar Sign road, with its hints of unsolved mystery. But she had quickly grown to love the broad, free Indian reservation, with its limitless miles of unfenced hills. She liked to turn off the road and gallop across the trackless ways, sometimes frightening rabbits and coyotes from the sagebrush. Several times she had startled antelope, and once her horse had shied at a rattlesnake coiled in the sunshine. The Indians she had learned to look upon as children. She had visited the cabins and lodges of some of those who lived near the ranch, and was not long in winning the esteem of the women who were finding the middle ground, between the simplicity of savage life and the complexities of civilization, something too much for mastery.

Lowell and Helen galloped in silence for miles along the road they had followed in the automobile not many days before. At the crest of a high ridge, Helen turned at right angles, and Lowell followed.

"There's a view over here I had appropriated for myself, but I'm willing to share it with you, seeing that this is your own particular reservation and you ought to know about everything it contains," said Helen.

The ridge dipped and then rose again, higher than before. The plains fell away on both sides—infinite miles of undulations. Straight ahead loomed the high blue wall of the mountains. They walked their horses, and finally stopped them altogether. The chattering of a few prairie dogs only served to intensify the great, mysterious silence.

"Sometimes the stillness seems to roll in on you here like a tide," said Helen. "I can positively feel it coming up these great slopes and blanketing everything. It seems to me that this ridge must have been used by Indian watchers in years gone by. I can imagine a scout standing here sending up smoke signals. And those little white puffs of clouds up there are the signals he sent into the sky."

"I think you belong in this country," Lowell answered smilingly.

"I'm sure I do. You remember when I first saw these plains and hills I told you the bigness frightened me a little when the sun brought it all out in detail. Well, it doesn't any more. Just to be unfettered in mind, and to live and breathe as part of all this vastness, would be ideal."

"That's where you're in danger of going to the other extreme," the agent replied. "You'll remember that I told you human companionship is as necessary as bacon and flour and salt in this country. You're more dependent on the people about you here, even if your nearest neighbor is five or ten miles away, than you would be in any apartment building in a big city. You might live and die there, and no one would be the wiser. Also you might get along tolerably well, while living alone. But you can't do it out here and keep a normal mental grip on life."

"My, what a lecture!" laughed the girl, though there was no merriment in her voice. "But it hardly applies to me, for the reason that I always depend upon my neighbors in the ordinary affairs of life. I'm sure I love to be sociable to my Indian neighbors, and even to their agent. Haven't I ridden away out here just to be sociable to you?"

"No dodging! I promised I wouldn't say anything more about the matters that have been disturbing you so, but that promise was contingent on your playing fair with me. I understand Bill Talpers has been causing you some annoyance, and you haven't said a word to me about it."

Helen flashed a startled glance at Lowell. He was impassive as her questioning eyes searched his face. Amazement and concern alternated in her features. Then she took refuge in a blaze of anger.

"I don't know how you found out about Talpers!" she cried. "It is true that he did cause a—a little annoyance, but that is all gone and forgotten. But I am not going to forget your impertinence quite so easily."

"My what?"

"Your impertinence?"

The girl was trembling with anger, or apprehension, and tapped her boot nervously with her quirt as she spoke.

"You've been lecturing me about various things," she went on, "and now you bring up Talpers as a sort of bugaboo to frighten me."

"You don't know Bill Talpers. If he has any sort of hold on you or on Willis Morgan, he'll try to break you both. He is as innocent of scruples as a lobo wolf."

"What hold could he possibly have on me—on us?"

She looked at Lowell defiantly as she asked the question, but he thought he detected a note of concern in her voice.

"I didn't say he had any hold. I merely pointed out that if he were given any opportunity he'd make life miserable for both of you."

Lowell did not add that Talpers, in a fit of rage and suspicion, augmented by strong drink, had hinted that Helen knew something of the murder. He had been inclined to believe that Talpers had merely been "fighting wild" when he made the veiled accusation—that the trader, being very evidently only partly recovered from a bout with his pet bottles, had made the first counter-assertion that had come into his head in the hope of provoking Lowell into a quarrel. But there was a quality of terror in the girl's voice which struck Lowell with chilling force. Something in his look must have caught Helen's attention, for her nervousness increased.

"You have no right to pillory me so," she said rapidly. "You have been perfectly impossible right along—that is, ever since this crime happened. You've been spying here and there—"

"Spying!"

"Yes, downright spying! You've been putting suspicion where it doesn't belong. Why, everybody believes the Indians did it—everybody but you. Probably some Indians did it who never have been suspected and never will be—not the Indians who are under suspicion now."

"That's just about what another party was telling me not long ago—that I was coddling the Indians and trying to fasten suspicion where it didn't rightfully belong."

"Who else told you that?"

"No less a person than Bill Talpers."

"There you go again, bringing in that cave man. Why do you keep talking to me about Talpers? I'm not afraid of him."

Most girls would have been on the verge of hysteria, Lowell thought, but, while Helen was plainly under a nervous strain, her self-command returned. The agent was in possession of some information—how much she did not know. Perhaps she could goad him into betraying the source of his knowledge.

"I know you're not afraid of Talpers," remarked Lowell, after a pause, "but at least give me the privilege of being afraid for you. I know Bill Talpers better than you do."

"What right have you to be afraid for me? I'm of age, and besides, I have a protector—a guardian—at the ranch."

Lowell was on the point of making some bitter reply about the undesirability of any guardianship assumed by Willis Morgan, squaw man, recluse, and recipient of common hatred and contempt. But he kept his counsel, and remarked, pleasantly:

"My rights are merely those of a neighbor—the right of one neighbor to help another."

"There are no rights of that sort where the other neighbor isn't asking any help and doesn't desire it."

"I'm not sure about your not needing it. Anyway, if you don't now, you may later."

The girl did not answer. The horses were standing close together, heads drooping lazily. Warm breezes came fitfully from the winds' playground below. The handkerchief at the girl's neck fluttered, and a strand of her hair danced and glistened in the sunshine. The graceful lines of her figure were brought out by her riding-suit. Lowell put his palm over the gloved hand on her saddle pommel. Even so slight a touch thrilled him.

"If a neighbor has no right to give advice," said Lowell, "let us assume that my unwelcome offerings have come from a man who is deeply in love with you. It's no great secret, anyway, as it seems to me that even the meadow-larks have been singing about it ever since we started on this ride."

The girl buried her face in her hands. Lowell put his arm about her waist, and she drooped toward him, but recovered herself with an effort. Putting his arm away, she said:

"You make matters harder and harder for me. Please forget what I have said and what you have said, and don't come to see me any more."

She spoke with a quiet intensity that amazed Lowell.

"Not come to see you any more! Why such an extreme sentence?"

"Because there is an evil spell on the Greek Letter Ranch. Everybody who comes there is certain to be followed by trouble—deep trouble."

The girl's agitation increased. There was terror in her face.

"Look here!" began Lowell. "This thing is beyond all promises of silence. I—"

"Don't ask what I mean!" said the girl. "You might find it awkward. You say you are in love with me?"

"I repeat it a thousand times."

"Well, you are the kind of man who will choose honor every time. I realize that much. Suppose you found that your love for me was bringing you in direct conflict with your duty?"

"I know that such a thing is impossible," broke in Lowell.

Helen smiled, bitterly.

"It is so far from being impossible that I am asking you to forget what you have said, and to forget me as well. There is so much of evil on the Greek Letter Ranch that the very soil there is steeped in it. I am going away, but I know its spell will follow me."

"You are going?" queried Lowell. "When?"

"When these men now charged with the murder are acquitted. They will be acquitted, will they not?"

The eager note in her question caught Lowell by surprise.

"No man can tell," he replied. "It's all as inscrutable as that mountain wall over there."

Helen shaded her eyes with her gauntleted hand as she looked in the direction indicated by Lowell. Black clouds were pouring in masses over the mountain-range. The sunshine was being blotted out, as if by some giant hand. The storm-clouds swept toward them as they turned the horses and started back along the ridge. A huge shadow, which Helen shudderingly likened to the sprawling figure of Talpers in the lamplight, raced toward them over the plains.

"There isn't a storm in all that blackness," Lowell assured her. "It's all shadow and no substance. Perhaps your fears will turn out that way."

The girl regarded him gravely.

"I've tried to hope as much, but it's no use, especially when you've felt the first actual buffetings of the storm."

The approaching cloud shadow seemed startlingly solid. The girl urged her horse into a gallop, and Lowell rode silently at her side. The shadow overtook them. Angry winds seemed to clutch at them from various angles, but no rain came from the cloud mass overhead. When they rode into the ranch yard, the sun was shining again. They dismounted near the barn, and Wong took the white horse. Lowell and the girl walked through the yard to the front gate, the agent leading his horse. As they passed near the porch there came through the open door that same chilling, sarcastic voice which stirred all the ire in Lowell's nature.

"Helen," the voice said, "that careless individual, Wong, must be reprimanded. He has mislaid one of my choicest volumes. Perhaps it would be better for you to attend to replacing the books on the shelves after this."

Every word was intended to humiliate, yet the voice was moderately pitched. There was even a slight drawl to it.

Lowell's face betrayed his anger as he glanced at the girl. He made a gesture of impatience, but Helen motioned to him, in warning.

"Some day you're going to let me take you away from this," he said grimly, looking at her with an intensity of devotion which brought the red to her cheeks. "Meantime, thanks for taking me out on that magic ridge. I'll never forget it."

"It will be better for you to forget everything," answered the girl.

Lowell was about to make a reply, when the voice came once more, cutting like a whiplash in a renewal of the complaint concerning the lost book. The girl turned, with a good-bye gesture, and ran indoors. Lowell led his horse outside the yard and rode toward Talpers's place, determined to have a few definite words with the trader.

When Lowell reached Talpers's, the usual knot of Indians was gathered on the front porch, with the customary collection of cowpunchers and ranchmen discussing matters inside the store.

"Bill ain't been here all the afternoon," said Talpers's clerk in answer to Lowell's question. "He sat around here for a while after you left this morning, and then he saddled up and took a pack-horse and hit off toward the reservation, but I don't know where he went or when he'll be back."

Lowell rode thoughtfully to the agency, trying in vain to bridge the gap between Talpers's cryptic utterances bearing on the murder, and the not less cryptic statements of Helen in the afternoon—an occupation which kept him unprofitably employed until far into the night.

CHAPTER X

Bill Talpers's return to sobriety was considerably hastened by alarm after the trader's words with Lowell. As long as matters were even between Bill Talpers and the girl, the trader figured that he could at least afford to let things rest. The letter in his possession was still a potent weapon. He could at least prevent the girl from telling what she seemed to know of the trader's connection with the murder. He had figured that the letter would be the means of bringing him a most engaging bride. It would have done so if he had not been such a fool as to drink too much. Talpers usually was a canny drinker, but when a man goes asking—or, in this case, demanding—a girl's hand in marriage, it is not to be wondered at if he oversteps the limit a trifle in the matter of fortifying himself with liquor. But in this case Bill realized that he had gone beyond all reasonable bounds. That fall had been disastrous in every way. She was clever and quick, that girl, or she never would have been able to turn an incident like that to such good advantage. Most girls would have sniveled in a corner, thought Bill, until he had regained his senses, but she started right in to look for that letter. He had been smart enough to leave the letter in the safe at the store, but she had found plenty in that watch!

Another thought buzzed disturbingly in Bill's head. How did she know just how much money had been taken from Sargent's body? Also, how did she know that the watch was Sargent's, seeing that it had no marks of identification on it? If there had been so much as a scratch on the thing, Talpers never would have worn it. She might have been making a wild guess about the watch, but she certainly was not guessing about the money. Her certainty in mentioning the amount had given Bill a chill of terror from which he was slow in recovering. Another thing that was causing him real agony of spirit was the prominence of Lowell in affairs at the Greek Letter Ranch. It would be easy enough to hold the girl in check with that letter. She would never dare tell the authorities how much she knew about Talpers, as Bill could drag her into the case by producing his precious documentary evidence. But the agent—how much was he learning in the course of his persistent searching, and from what angle was he going to strike? Would the girl provide him with information which she might not dare give to others? Women were all weaklings, thought Bill, unable to keep any sort of a secret from a sympathetic male ear, especially when that ear belonged to as handsome a young fellow as the Indian agent! Probably she would be telling the agent everything on his next trip to the ranch. Bill had been watching, but he had not seen the young upstart from the agency go past, and neither had Bill's faithful clerk. But the visit might be made any day, and Talpers's connection with the tragedy on the Dollar Sign road might at almost any hour be falling into the possession of Lowell, whose activity in running down bootleggers had long ago earned him Bill's hatred.

Something would have to be done, without delay, to get the girl where she would not be making a confidant of Lowell or any one else. Scowlingly Bill thought over one plan after another, and rejected each as impractical. Finally, by a process of elimination, he settled on the only course that seemed practical. A broad fist, thudding into a leather-like palm, indicated that the Talpers mind had been made up. With his dark features expressing grim resolve, Bill threw a burden of considerable size on his best pack-animal. This operation he conducted alone in the barn, rejecting his clerk's proffer of assistance. Then he saddled another horse, and, without telling his clerk anything concerning his prospective whereabouts or the length of his trip, started off across the prairie. He often made such excursions, and his clerk had learned not to ask questions. Diplomacy in such matters was partly what the clerk was paid for. A good fellow to work for was Bill Talpers if no one got too curiously inclined. One or two clerks had been disciplined on account of inquisitiveness, and they would not be as beautiful after the Talpers methods had been applied, but they had gained vastly in experience. Some day he would do even more for this young Indian agent. Bill's cracked lips were stretched in a grin of satisfaction at the very thought.

The trader traveled swiftly toward the reservation. He often boasted that he got every ounce that was available in horseflesh. Traveling with a pack-horse was little handicap to him. Horses instinctively feared him. More than one he had driven to death without so much as touching the straining animal with whip or spur. Nothing gave Bill such acute satisfaction as the knowledge that he had roused fear in any creature.

With the sweating pack-animal close at the heels of his saddle pony, Talpers rode for hours across the plains. Seemingly he paid no attention to the changes in the landscape, yet his keen eyes, buried deeply beneath black brows, took in everything. He saw the cloud masses come tumbling over the mountains, but, like Lowell, he knew that the drought was not yet to be ended. The country became more broken, and the grade so pronounced that the horses were compelled to slacken their pace. The pleasant green hills gave place to imprisoning mesas, with red sides that looked like battlements. Beyond these lay the foothills—so close that they covered the final slopes of the mountains.

It was a lonely country, innocent of fences. The cattle that ran here were as wild as deer and almost as fleet as antelope. Twice a year the Indians rounded up their range possessions, but many of these cattle had escaped the far-flung circles of riders. They had become renegades and had grown old and clever. At the sight of a human being they would gallop away in the sage and greasewood.

Once Talpers saw the gleam of a wagon-top which indicated the presence of a wolf hunter in the employ of the leasers who were running cattle on the reservations and who suffered much from the depredations of predatory animals. By working carefully around a hill, the trader continued on his way without having been seen.

Passing the flanking line of mesas, Bill pushed his way up a watercourse between two foothills. The going became rougher, and all semblance of a trail was lost, yet the trader went on unhesitatingly. The slopes leading to the creek became steeper and were covered with pine and quaking aspen, instead of the bushy growths of the plains. The stream foamed over rocks, and its noise drowned the sound of the horses' hoofs as the animals scrambled over the occasional stretches of loose shale. With the dexterity of the born trailsman, Talpers wormed his way along the stream when it seemed as if further progress would be impossible. In a tiny glade, with the mountain walls rising precipitously for hundreds of feet, Talpers halted and gave three shrill whistles. An answer came from the other end of the glade, and in a few minutes Talpers was removing pack and saddle in Jim McFann's camp.

Since his escape from jail the half-breed had been hiding in this mountain fastness. Talpers had supplied him with "grub" and weapons. He had moved camp once in a while for safety's sake, but had felt little fear of capture. As a trailer McFann had few equals, and he knew every swale in the prairie and every nook in the mountains on the reservation.

Talpers brought out a bottle, which McFann seized eagerly.

"There's plenty more in the pack," said the trader, "so drink all you want. Don't offer me none, as I am kind o' taperin' off."

"Did you see any Indian police on the way?" asked the half-breed.

"No—nothin' but Wolfer Joe's wagon, 'way off in the hills. I guess the police ain't lookin' for you very hard. That ain't the fault of the agent, though," added Talpers meaningly. "He's promised he'll have you back in Tom Redmond's hands in less'n a week."

The half-breed scowled and muttered an oath as he took another drink. Talpers had told the lie in order to rouse McFann's antagonism toward Lowell, and he was pleased to see that his statement had been accepted at face value.

"But that ain't the worst for you, nor for me either," went on the trader. "That girl at the Greek Letter Ranch knows that you and me took the watch from the man on the Dollar Sign road."

"How did she know that?" exclaimed McFann in amazement.

"That's somethin' she won't tell, but she knows that you and me was there, and that the story you told in court ain't straight. I'm satisfied she ain't told any one else—not yet."

"Do you think she will tell any one?"

"I'm sure of it. You see, she sorter sprung this thing on me when I was havin' a little argyment about her marryin' me. She got spiteful and come at me with the statement that the watch I was wearin' belonged to that feller Sargent."

Bill did not add anything about the money. It was not going to do to let the half-breed know he had been defrauded.

McFann squatted by the fire, the bottle in his hand and his gaze on Talpers's face.

"She mentioned both of us bein' there," went on the trader. "She give the details in a way that I'll admit took me off my feet. It's an awkward matter—in fact, it's a hangin' matter—for both of us, if she tells. You know how clost they was to lynchin' you, over there at White Lodge, with nothin' so very strong against you. If that gang ever hears about us and this watch of Sargent's, we'll be hung on the same tree."

Talpers played heavily on the lynching, because he knew the fear of the mob had become an obsession with McFann. He noticed the half-breed's growing uneasiness, and played his big card.

"I spent a long time thinkin' the hull thing over," said Talpers, "and I've come to the conclusion that this girl is sure to tell the Indian agent all she knows, and the best thing for us to do is to get her out of the way before she puts the noose around our necks."

"Why will she tell the Indian agent?"

"Because he's callin' pretty steady at the ranch, and he's made her think he's the only friend she's got around here. And as soon as he finds out, we might as well pick out our own rope neckties, Jim. It's goin' to take quick action to save us, but you're the one to do it."

"What do you want me to do?" asked McFann suspiciously.

"Well, you're the best trailer and as good a shot as there is in this part of the country. All that's necessary is for you to drop around the ranch and—well, sort of make that girl disappear."

"How do you mean?"

Talpers rose and came closer to McFann.

"I mean kill her!" he said with an oath. "Nothin' else is goin' to do. You can do it without leavin' a track. Willis Morgan or that Chinaman never'll see you around. Nobody else but the agent ever stops at the Greek Letter Ranch. It's the only safe way. If she ever tells, Jim, you'll never come to trial. You'll be swingin' back and forth somewheres to the music of the prairie breeze. You know the only kind of fruit that grows on these cotton woods out here."

Jim McFann had always been pliable in Talpers's hands. Talpers had profited most by the bootlegging operations carried on by the pair, though Jim had done most of the dangerous work. Whenever Jim needed supplies, the trader furnished them. To be sure, he charged them off heavily, so there was little cash left from the half-breed's bootlegging operations. Talpers shrewdly figured that the less cash he gave Jim, the more surely he could keep his hold on the half-breed. McFann had grown used to his servitude. Talpers appeared to him in the guise of the only friend he possessed among white and red.

Jim rose slowly to his moccasined feet.

"I guess you're right, Bill," he said. "I'll do what you say."

The trader's eyes glowed with satisfaction. The desire for revenge had come uppermost in his heart. The girl at the ranch had outwitted him in some way which he could not understand. Twenty-four hours ago he had confidently figured on numbering her among the choicest chattels in the possession of William Talpers. But now he regarded her with a hatred born of fear. The thought of what she could do to him, merely by speaking a few careless words about that watch and money, drove all other thoughts from Talpers's mind. Jim McFann could be made a deadly and certain instrument for insuring the safety of the Talpers skin. One shot from the half-breed's rifle, either through a cabin window or from some sagebrush covert near the ranch, and the trader need have no further fears about being connected with the Dollar Sign murder.

"I thought you'd see it in the right light, Jim," approved Talpers. "It won't be any trick at all to get her. She rides out a good deal on that white horse."

Jim McFann did not answer. He had begun preparations for his trip. Swiftly and silently the half-breed saddled his horse, which had been hidden in a near-by thicket. From the supply of liquor in Talpers's pack, Jim took a bottle, which he was thrusting into his saddle pocket when the trader snatched it away.

"You've had enough, Jim," growled Talpers. "You do the work that's cut out for you, and you can have all I've brought to camp. I'll be here waitin' for you."

McFann scowled.

"All right," he said sullenly, "but it seems as if a man ought to have lots for a job like this."

"After it's all done," said Talpers soothingly, "you can have all the booze you want, Jim. And one thing more," called the trader as McFann rode away, "remember it ain't goin' to hurt either of us if you get a chance to put the Indian agent away on this same little trip."

Jim McFann waved an assenting sign as he disappeared in the trees, and the trader went back to the camp-fire to await the half-breed's return. He hoped McFann would find the agent at the Greek Letter Ranch and would kill Lowell as well as the girl. But, if there did not happen to be any such double stroke of luck in prospect, the removal of the Indian agent could be attended to later on.

When he reached the mesas beyond the foothills, the half-breed turned away from the stream and struck off toward the left. He kept a sharp lookout for Indian police as he traveled, but saw nothing to cause apprehension. Night was fast coming on when he reached the ridge on which Lowell and Helen had stood a few hours before. Avoiding the road, the half-breed made his way to a gulch near the ranch, where he tied his horse. Cautiously he approached the ranch-house. The kitchen door was open and Wong was busy with the dishes. The other doors were shut and shades were drawn in the windows. Making his way back to the gulch, the half-breed rolled up in his blanket and slept till daybreak, when he took up a vantage-point near the house and waited developments. Shortly after breakfast Wong came out to the barn and saddled the white horse for Helen. The half-breed noticed with satisfaction that the girl rode directly toward the reservation instead of following the road that led to the agency. Hastily securing his horse the half-breed skirted the ranch and located the girl's trail on the prairie. Instead of following it he ensconced himself comfortably in some aspens at the bottom of a draw, confident that the girl would return by the same trail.

If McFann had continued on Helen's trail he would have followed her to an Indian ranch not far away. A tattered tepee or two snuggled against a dilapidated cabin. The owner of the ranch was struggling with tuberculosis. His wife was trying to run the place and to bring up several children, whose condition had aroused the mother instinct in Helen. Though she had found her first efforts regarded with suspicion, Helen had persisted, until she had won the confidence of mother and children. Her visits were frequent, and she had helped the family so materially that she had astonished the field matron, an energetic woman who covered enormous distances in the saddle in the fulfillment of duties which would soon wear out a settlement worker.

The half-breed smoked uneasily, his rifle across his knees. Two hours passed, but he did not stir, so confident was he that Helen would return by the way she had followed in departing from the ranch.

McFann's patience was rewarded, and he tossed away his cigarette with a sigh of satisfaction when Helen's voice came to him from the top of the hill. She was singing a nonsense song from the nursery, and, astride behind her saddle and clinging to her waist, was a wide-eyed Indian girl of six years, enjoying both the ride and the singing.

Here was a complication upon which the half-breed had not counted. In fact, during his hours of waiting Jim had begun to look at matters in a different light. It was necessary to get Helen away, where she could not possibly tell what she knew, but why not hide her in the mountains? Or, if stronger methods were necessary, let Talpers attend to them himself? For the first time since he had come under Talpers's domination, Jim McFann was beginning to weaken. As the girl came singing down the hillside, Jim peered uneasily through the bushes. Talpers had shoved him into a job that simply could not be carried out—at least not without whiskey. If Bill had let him bring all he wanted to drink, perhaps things could have been done as planned.

Whatever was done would have to be accomplished quickly, as the white horse, with its double burden, was getting close. Jim sighted once or twice along his rifle barrel. Then he dropped the weapon into the hollow of his arm, and, leading his horse, stepped in front of Helen.

The parley was brief. McFann sent the youngster scurrying along the back trail, after a few threats in Indian tongue, which were dire enough to seal the child's lips in fright. Helen was startled at first when the half-breed halted her, but her composure soon returned. She had no weapon, nor would she have attempted to use one in any event, as she knew the half-breed was famous for his quickness and cleverness with firearms. Nor could anything be gained by attempting to ride him down in the trail. She did not ask any questions, for she felt they would be futile.

The half-breed was surprised at the calmness with which matters were being taken. With singular ease and grace—another gift from his Indian forbears—Jim slid into his saddle, and, seizing the white horse by the bridle, turned the animal around and started it up the trail beside him. In a few minutes Jim had found his trail of the evening before, and was working swiftly back toward the mountains. When Helen slyly dropped her handkerchief, as an aid to any one who might follow, the half-breed quietly turned back and, after picking it up, informed her that he would kill her if she tried any more such tricks. Realizing the folly of any further attempts to outwit the half-breed, Helen rode silently on. Not once did McFann strike across a ridge. Imprisoning slopes seemed to be shutting them in without surcease, and Helen looked in vain for any aid.

As they approached the foothills, and the travel increased in difficulty, McFann told Helen to ride close behind him. He glanced around occasionally to see that she was obeying orders. The old white horse struggled gamely after the half-breed's wiry animal, and McFann was compelled to wait only once or twice. Meanwhile Helen had thought over the situation from every possible angle, and had concluded to go ahead and not make any effort to thwart the half-breed. She knew that the reservation was more free from crime than the counties surrounding it. She also knew that it would not be long before the agent was informed of her disappearance, and that the Indian police—trailers who were the half-breed's equal in threading the ways of the wilderness—would soon be on McFann's tracks. After her first shock of surprise she had little fear of McFann. The thought that disturbed her most of all was—Talpers. She knew of the strange partnership of the men. Likewise she felt that McFann would not have embarked upon any such crime alone. The thought of Talpers recurred so steadily that the lithe figure of the half-breed in front of her seemed to change into the broad, almost misshapen form of the trader.

The first real fear that had come to her since the strange journey began surged over Helen when McFann led the way into the glade where he had been camped, and she saw a dreaded and familiar figure stooped over a small fire, engaged in frying bacon. But there was nothing of triumph in Talpers's face as he straightened up and saw Helen. Amazement flitted across the trader's features, succeeded by consternation.

"Now you've done it and done it right!" exclaimed the trader, with a shower of oaths directed at Jim McFann. "Didn't have the nerve to shoot at a purty face like that, did you? Git her into that tent while you and me set down and figger out what we're goin' to do!"

The half-breed helped Helen dismount and told her to go to his tent, a small, pyramid affair at one end of the glade. Jim fastened the flaps on the outside and went back to the camp-fire, where Talpers was storming up and down like a madman. Helen, seated on McFann's blanket roll, heard their voices rising and falling, the half-breed apparently defending himself and Talpers growing louder and more accusative. Finally, when the trader's rage seemed to have spent itself somewhat, the tent flaps were opened and Jim McFann thrust some food into Helen's hands. She ate the bacon and biscuits, as the long ride had made her hungry. Then Talpers roughly ordered her out of the tent. He and the half-breed had been busy packing and saddling. They added the tent and its contents to their packs. Telling Helen to mount the white horse once more, Talpers took the lead, and, with the silent and sullen half-breed bringing up the rear, the party started off along a trail much rougher than the one that had been followed by McFann and the girl in the morning.

CHAPTER XI

It was fortunate that Helen had accustomed herself to long rides, as otherwise she could not have undergone the experiences of the next few hours in the saddle. All semblance of a trail seemed to end a mile or so beyond the camp. The ride became a succession of scrambles across treacherous slides of shale, succeeded by plunges into apparently impenetrable walls of underbrush and low-hanging trees. The general course of the river was followed. At times they had climbed to such a height that the stream was merely a white line beneath them, and its voice could not be heard. Then they would descend and cross and recross the stream. The wild plunges across the torrent became matters of torture to Helen. The horses slipped on the boulders. Water dashed over the girl's knees, and each ford became more difficult, as the stream became more swollen, owing to the melting of near-by snowbanks. One of the pack-horses fell and lay helplessly in the stream until it was fairly dragged to its feet. The men cursed volubly as they worked over the animal and readjusted the wet pack, which had slipped to one side.

After an hour or two of travel the half-breed took Talpers's place in the lead, the trader bringing up the rear behind Helen and the pack-horses. Two bald mountain-peaks began to loom startlingly near. The stream ran between the peaks, being fed by the snows on either slope. As the altitude became more pronounced the horses struggled harder at their work. The white horse was showing the stamina that was in him. Helen urged him to his task, knowing the folly of attempting to thwart the wishes of her captors. They passed a slope where a forest fire had swept in years gone by. Wild raspberry bushes had grown in profusion among the black, sentinel-like trunks of dead trees. The bushes tore her riding-suit and scratched her hands, but she uttered no complaint.

Under any other circumstances Helen would have found much in the ride to overcome its discomforts. The majesty of the scenery impressed itself upon her mind, troubled as she was. Silence wrapped the two great peaks like a mantle. An eagle swung lazily in midair between the granite spires. Here was another plane of existence where the machinations of men seemed to matter little. Almost indifferent to her discomforts Helen struggled on, mechanically keeping her place in line. The half-breed looked back occasionally, and even went so far as to take her horse by the bridle and help the animal up an unusually hard slope.

When it became apparent that further progress was an impossibility unless the pack-horses were abandoned, the half-breed turned aside, and, after a final desperate scramble up the mountain-side, the party entered a fairly open, level glade. Helen dismounted with the others.

"We're goin' to camp here for a while," announced Talpers, after a short whispered conference with the half-breed. "You might as well make yourself as comfortable as you can, but remember one thing—you'll be shot if you try to get away or if you make any signals."

Helen leaned back against a tree-trunk, too weary to make answer, and Talpers went to the assistance of McFann, who was taking off the packs and saddles. The horses were staked out near at hand, where they could get their fill of the luxuriant grass that carpeted the mountain-side here. McFann brought water from a spring near at hand, and the trader set out some food from one of the packs, though it was decided not to build a fire to cook anything. Helen ate biscuits and bacon left from the previous meal. While she was eating, McFann put up the little tent. Then, after another conference with Talpers, the half-breed climbed a rock which jutted out of the shoulder of the mountain not far from them. His lithe figure was silhouetted against the reddening sky. Helen wondered, as she looked up at him, if the rock had been used for sentinel purposes in years gone by. Her reflections were broken in upon by Talpers.

"That tent is yours," said the trader, in a low voice. "But before you turn in I've got a few words to say to you. You haven't seemed to be as much afraid of me on this trip as you was the other night at your cabin."

"There's no reason why I should be," said Helen quietly. "You don't dare harm me for several reasons."

"What are they?" sneered Talpers.

"Well, one reason is—Jim McFann. All I have to do to cause your partnership to dissolve at once is to tell Jim that you found that money on the man who was murdered and didn't divide."

Talpers winced.

"Furthermore, this business has practically made an outlaw of you. It all depends on your treatment of me. I'm the collateral that may get you back into the good graces of society."

Talpers wiped the sweat beads off his forehead.

"You don't want to be too sure of yourself," he growled, though with so much lack of assurance that Helen was secretly delighted. "You want to remember," went on the trader threateningly, "that any time we want to put a bullet in you, we can make our getaway easy enough. The only thing for you to do is to keep quiet and see that you mind orders."

Talpers ended the interview hastily when McFann came down from the rock. The men talked together, after shutting Helen in the tent and reiterating that she would be watched and that the first attempt to escape would be fatal. Helen flung herself down on the blankets and watched the fading lights of evening as they were reflected on the canvas. She could hear the low voices of Talpers and McFann, hardly distinguishable from the slight noises made by the wind in the trees. The moon cast the shadows of branches on the canvas, and the noise of the stream, far below, came fitfully to Helen's ears. She was more at ease in mind than at any other time since Jim McFann had confronted her with his rifle over his arm. She felt that Talpers was the moving spirit in her kidnaping. She did not know how near her knowledge of the trader's implication in the Dollar Sign tragedy had brought her to death. Nor did she know that Talpers's rage over Jim McFann's weakening had been so great that the trader had nearly snatched up his rifle and shot his partner dead when the half-breed brought Helen into camp.

As a matter of fact, when Talpers had realized that Jim McFann had failed in his mission of assassination, the trader had been consumed with alternate rage and fear. A kidnaping had been the last thing in the world in the trader's thoughts. Assassination, with some one else doing the work, was much the better way. Running off with womenfolk could not be made a profitable affair, but here was the girl thrown into his hands by fate. It would not do to let her go. Perhaps a way out of the mess could be thought over. McFann could be made to bear the brunt in some way. Meantime the best thing to do was to get as far into the hills as possible. McFann could outwit the Indian police. He had been doing it right along. He had fooled them during long months of bootlegging. Since his escape from jail the police had redoubled their efforts to capture McFann, but he had gone right on fooling them. If worst came to worst, McFann and he could make their getaway alone, first putting the girl where she would never tell what she knew about them. Across the mountains there was a little colony of law-breakers that had long been after Talpers as a leader. He had helped them in a good many ways, these outlaws, particularly in rustling cattle from the reservation herds. It was Bill Talpers who had evolved the neat little plan of changing the ID brand of the Interior Department to the "two-pole pumpkin" brand, which was done merely by extending another semicircle to the left of the "I" and connecting that letter and the "D" at top and bottom, thus making two perpendicular lines in a flattened circle.

The returns from his interest in the gang's rustling operations had been far more than Bill had ever secured from his store. In fact, storekeeping was played out. Bill never would have kept it up except for the opportunity it gave him to find out what was going on. To be sure, he should have played safe and kept away from such things as that affair on the Dollar Sign road. But he could have come clear even there if it had not been for the uncanny knowledge possessed by that girl. The thought of what would happen if she took a notion to tell McFann how he had been "double-crossed" by his partner gave Talpers something approaching a chill. The half-breed was docile enough as long as he thought he was being fairly dealt with. But once let him find out that he had been unfairly treated, all the Indian in him would come to the surface with a rush! Fortunately the girl was proving herself to be close-mouthed. She had traveled for hours with the half-breed without telling him of Talpers's perfidy. Now Bill would see to it that she got no chance to talk with McFann. The half-breed was too tender-hearted where women were concerned. That much had been proved when he had fallen down in the matter of the work he had been sent out to do. If she had a chance the girl might even persuade him to let her escape, which was not going to do at all. If anybody was to be left holding the sack at the end of the adventure, it would not be Bill Talpers!

With various stratagems being brought to mind, only to be rejected one after another, Talpers watched the tent until midnight, the half-breed sleeping near at hand. Then Bill turned in while McFann kept watch. As for Helen, she slept the sleep of exhaustion until wakened by the touch of daylight on the canvas.

With senses preternaturally sharpened, as they generally are during one's first hours in the wilderness, Helen listened. She heard Talpers stirring about among the horses. It was evident that he was alarmed about something, as he was pulling the picket-pins and bringing the animals closer to the center of the glade. McFann had been looking down the valley from the sentinel rock. She did not hear him come into camp, as the half-breed always moved silently through underbrush that would betray the presence of any one less skilled in woodcraft. She heard his monosyllabic answers to Talpers's questions. Then Bill himself pushed his way through the underbrush and climbed the rock. When he returned to the camp he came to the tent.

"I don't mind tellin' you that Plenty Buffalo is out there on the trail, with an Injun policeman or two. That young agent don't seem to have had nerve enough to come along," said Talpers, producing a small rope. "I'll have to tie your hands awhile, just to make sure you don't try gittin' away. I'm goin' to tell 'em that at the first sign of rushin' the camp you're goin' to be shot. What's more I'm goin' to mean what I tell 'em."

Talpers tied Helen's hands behind her. He left the flaps of the tent open as he picked up his rifle and returned to McFann, who was sitting on a log, composedly enough, keeping watch of the other end of the glade where the trail entered. Helen sank to her knees, with her back to the rear of the tent, so she could command a better view. The tent had been staked down securely around the edges, so there was no opportunity for her to crawl under.

Apparently the two men in the glade, as Helen saw them through the inverted V of the open tent flaps, were most peacefully inclined. They sat smoking and talking, and, from all outward appearances, might have been two hunters talking over the day's prospects. Suddenly they sprang to their feet, and, with rifles in readiness, looked toward the trail, which was hidden from Helen's vision.

"Don't come any nearer, Plenty Buffalo," called Talpers, in Indian language. "If you try to rush the camp, the first thing we'll do is to kill this girl. The only thing for you to do is to go back."

Then followed a short colloquy, Helen being unable to hear Plenty Buffalo's voice.

Evidently he was well down the trail, hidden in the trees, and was making no further effort to approach. The men sat down again, watching the trail and evidently figuring out their plan of escape. There was no means of scaling the mountain wall behind them. Horses could not possibly climb that steep slope, covered with such a tangle of trees and undergrowth, but it was possible to proceed farther along the upper edge of the valley until finally timber-line was reached, after which the party could drop over the divide into the happy little kingdom just off the reservation where a capable man with the branding-iron was always welcome and where the authorities never interfered.

Helen listened for another call from Plenty Buffalo, but the minutes dragged past and no summons came. The silence of the forest became almost unbearable. The men sat uneasily, casting occasional glances back at the tent, and making sure that Helen was remaining quiet. Finally Plenty Buffalo called again. There was another brief parley and Talpers renewed his threats. While the talk was going on, Helen heard a slight noise behind her. Turning her head, she saw the point of a knife cutting a long slit in the back of the tent. Then Fire Bear's dark face peered in through the opening.

The Indian's long brown arm reached forth and the bonds at Helen's wrists were cut. The arm disappeared through the slit in the canvas, beckoning as it did so. Helen backed slowly toward the opening that had been made.

The talk between Plenty Buffalo and Talpers was still going on. Helen waited until both men had glanced around at her. Then, as they turned their heads once more toward Plenty Buffalo's hiding-place, she half leaped, half fell through the opening in the tent. A strong hand kept her from falling and guided her swiftly through the underbrush back of the tent. Her face was scratched by the bushes that swung back as the half-naked Indian glided ahead of her, but, in almost miraculous fashion, she found a traversable path opened. Torn and bleeding, she flung herself behind a rock, just as a shout from the camp told that her disappearance had been discovered. There was a crashing of pursuers through the underbrush, but a gun roared a warning, almost in Helen's ear.

The shot was fired by Lowell, who, hatless and with torn clothing, had followed Fire Bear within a short distance of the camp. Helen crouched against the rock, while Lowell stood over her firing into the forest tangle. Fire Bear stood nonchalantly beside Lowell. Helen noticed, wonderingly, that there was not a scratch on the Indian's naked shoulders, yet Lowell's clothes were torn, and blood dripped from his palms where he had followed Fire Bear along the seemingly impassable way back of the camp.

One or two answering shots were fired, but evidently Talpers and his companion were afraid of an attack by Plenty Buffalo, so no pursuit was attempted.

The Indian turned, and, motioning for Lowell and Helen to follow, disappeared in the undergrowth along the trail which he and the agent had made while Plenty Buffalo was attracting the attention of Talpers and the half-breed. Helen tried to rise, but the sudden ending of the mental strain proved unnerving. She leaned against the rock with her eyes closed and her body limp. Lowell lifted her to her feet, almost roughly. For a moment she stood with Lowell's arms about her and his kisses on her face. Her whiteness alarmed him.

"Tell me you haven't been harmed," he cried. "If you have—"

"Just these scratches and a good riding-suit in tatters," she answered, as she drew away from him with a reassuring smile.

Lowell's brow cleared, and he laughed gleefully, as he picked up his rifle.

"Well, there's just one more hard scramble ahead," he replied, "and perhaps some more tatters to add to what both of us have. I'd carry you, but the best I can do is to help you over some of the more difficult places. Fire Bear has started. Have you strength enough to try to follow?"

He led her along the trail taken by Fire Bear—a trail in name only. The Indian had waited for them a few yards away. How much he had seen and heard when Lowell held her in his arms Helen could only surmise, but the thought sent the blood into her cheeks with a rush.

It was as Lowell had said—another scramble. At times it seemed as if she could not go on, but always at the right time Lowell gave the necessary help that enabled her to surmount some seemingly impassable obstacle. As for Fire Bear, he made his way over huge rocks and along steep pitches of shale with the ease of a serpent. At last the way became somewhat less difficult to traverse, and, when they came out on the trail by the stream, Helen realized that the tax on her physical resources was ended.

A short distance down the trail they met Plenty Buffalo with two Indian policemen. One of the police had been wounded in the arm by a shot from Talpers. The trader and McFann had hurriedly packed and made their escape, leaving the white horse, which Plenty Buffalo had brought for Helen.

After a hasty examination of the Indian's arm it was decided to hurry back to the agency for aid.

"I've sent out a call for more of the Indian police," said Lowell. "They'll probably be there when we get back to the agency. We just picked up what help we could find when we got word of your disappearance."

When Helen looked around for Fire Bear, the Indian had disappeared.

"We never could have done anything without Fire Bear," said Lowell, as he swung into the saddle preparatory to the homeward ride. "He is the greatest trailer I ever saw. Probably he's gone back to his camp, now that this interruption in his religious ceremonies is over."

Plenty Buffalo led the way back to the agency with the wounded policeman. Lowell had examined the man's injury and was satisfied that it was only superficial. The policeman himself took matters with true Indian philosophy, and galloped on with Plenty Buffalo, the most unconcerned member of the party.

Lowell rode with Helen, letting the others go on ahead after they had reached the open country beyond the foothills. He explained the circumstances of the rescue—how Wong had brought a note signed "Willis

Morgan," telling of Helen's disappearance. At the same time Fire Bear had come to the agency with the news that one of his young men had seen McFann and Helen riding toward the mountains. Fire Bear was convinced that something was wrong and had lost no time in telling Lowell. With Plenty Buffalo and one or two Indian policemen who happened to be at the agency, a posse was hurriedly made up. Fire Bear took the trail and followed it so swiftly and unerringly that the party was almost within striking distance of the fugitives by night-fall. A conference had been held, and it was decided to let Plenty Buffalo parley with Talpers and McFann from the trail, while Fire Bear attempted the seemingly impossible task of entering the camp from the side toward the mountain.

Helen was silent during most of the ride to the agency. Lowell ascribed her silence to a natural reaction from the physical and mental strain of recent hours. After reaching the agency he saw that the wounded policeman was properly taken care of. Then Lowell and Helen started for the Greek Letter Ranch in the agent's car, leaving her horse to be brought over by one of the agency employees.

"Do you intend to go back and take up the chase for Talpers and McFann?" asked Helen.

"Of course! Just as soon as I can get more of the Indian police together."

"But they'll hardly be taken alive, will they?"

"Perhaps not."

"That means that blood will be shed on my account," declared Helen. "I'll not have it! I don't want those men captured! What if I refuse to testify against them?"

Lowell looked at her in amazement. Then it came to him overwhelmingly that here was the murder mystery stalking between them once more, like a ghost. He recalled Talpers's broad hint that Helen knew something of the case, and that if Bill Talpers were dragged into the Dollar Sign affair the girl at the Greek Letter Ranch would be dragged in also.

"There is no need of the outside world knowing anything about this," went on Helen. "The Indian police do not report to any one but you, do they?"

"No. Their lips are sealed so far as their official duties are concerned."

"Fire Bear will have nothing to say?"

"He has probably forgotten it by this time in his religious fervor."

"Then I ask you to let these men go."

"If you will not appear against them," said Lowell, "I can't see that anything will be gained by bringing them in. But probably it would be a good thing to exterminate them on the tenable ground that they are general menaces to the welfare of society."

The girl's troubled expression returned.

"On one condition I will send word to Talpers that he may return," went on Lowell. "That condition is that you rescind your order excluding me from the Greek Letter Ranch. If Talpers comes back I've got to be allowed to drop around to see that you are not spirited away."

CHAPTER XII

Talpers was back in his store in two days. Lowell sent word that the trader might return. At first Talpers was hesitant and suspicious. There was a lurking fear in his mind that the agent had some trick in view, but, as life took its accustomed course, Bill resumed his domineering attitude about the store. A casual explanation that he had been buying some cattle was enough to explain his absence.

Bill's recent experiences had caused him to regard the agent with new hatred, not unmixed with fear. The obvious thing for Lowell to have done was to have rushed more men on the trail and captured Talpers and McFann before they crossed the reservation line. It could have been done, with Fire Bear doing the trailing. Even the half-breed admitted that much. But, instead of carrying out such a programme, the agent had sent Fire Bear and Plenty Buffalo with word that the trader might come back—that no prosecution was intended.

Clearly enough such an unusual proceeding indicated that the girl was still afraid on account of the letter, and had persuaded the agent to abandon the chase. There was the key to the whole situation—the letter! Bill determined to guard it more closely than ever. He opened his safe frequently to see that it was there.

As a whole, then, things were not breaking so badly, Bill figured. To be sure, it would have cleared things permanently if Jim McFann had done as he had been told, instead of weakening in such unexpected and absurd fashion. Bringing that girl into camp, as Jim had done, had given Talpers the most unpleasant surprise of his life. He had come out of the affair luckily. The letter was what had done it all. He would lie low and keep an eye on affairs from now on. McFann would have no difficulty in shifting for himself out in the sagebrush, now that he was alone. Bill would see that he got grub and even a little whiskey occasionally, but there would be no more assignments for him in which women were concerned, for the half-breed had too tender a heart for his own good!

The Indian agent stopped at Bill's store occasionally, on his way to and from the Greek Letter Ranch. Their conversation ran mostly to trade and minor affairs of life in general. Even the weather was fallen back upon in case some one happened to be within earshot, which was usually the case, as Bill's store was seldom empty. No one who heard them would suspect that the men were watching, weighing, and fathoming each other with all the nicety at individual command. Talpers was always wondering just how much the Indian agent knew, and Lowell was saying to himself:

"This scoundrel has some knowledge in his possession which vitally affects the young woman I love. Also he is concerned, perhaps deeply, in the murder on the Dollar Sign road. Yet he has fortified himself so well in his villainy that he feels secure."

For all his increased feeling of security, Talpers was wise enough to let the bottle alone and also to do no boasting. Likewise he stuck faithfully to his store—so faithfully that it became a matter of public comment.

"If Bill sticks much closer to this store he's goin' to fall into a decline," said Andy Wolters, who had been restored to favor in the circle of cowpunchers that lolled about Talpers's place. "He's gettin' a reg'lar prison pallor now. He used to be hittin' the trail once in a while, but nowadays he's hangin' around that post-office section as if he expected a letter notifyin' him that a rich uncle had died."

"Mebbe he's afraid of travelin' these parts since that feller was killed on the Dollar Sign," suggested another cowboy. "Doggoned if I don't feel a little shaky myself sometimes when I'm ridin' that road alone at night. Looks like some of them Injuns ought to have been hung for that murder, right off the reel, and then folks'd feel a lot easier in their minds."

The talk then would drift invariably to the subject of the murder and the general folly of the court in allowing Fire Bear to go on the Indian agent's recognizance. But Talpers, though he heard the chorus of denunciation from the back of the store, and though he was frequently called upon for an opinion, never could be drawn into the conversation. He bullied his clerk as usual, and once in a while swept down, in a storm of baseless anger, upon some unoffending Indian, just to show that Bill Talpers was still a man to be feared, but for the most part he waited silently, with the confidence of a man who holds a winning hand at cards.

The same days that saw Talpers's confidence returning were days of dissatisfaction to Lowell. He felt that he was being constantly thwarted. He would have preferred to give his entire attention to the murder mystery, but details of reservation management crowded upon him in a way that made avoidance impossible. Among his duties Lowell found that he must act as judge and jury in many cases that came up. There were domestic difficulties to be straightened out, and thieves and brawlers to be sentenced. Likewise there was occasional flotsam, cast up from the human sea outside the reservation, which required attention.

One of those reminders of the outer world was brought in by an Indian policeman. The stranger was a rough-looking individual, to all appearances a harmless tramp, who had been picked up "hoofing it" across the reservation.

The Indian policeman explained, through the interpreter, that he had found the wanderer near a sub-agency, several miles away—that he had shown a disposition to fight, and had only been cowed by the prompt presentation of a revolver at his head.

"Why, you 're no tramp—you're a yeggman," said Lowell to the prisoner, interrupting voluble protestations of innocence. "You're one of the gentry that live off small post-offices and banks. I'll bet you've stolen stamps enough in your career to keep the Post-Office Department going six months. And you've given heart disease to no end of stockholders in small banks—prosperous citizens who have had to make good the losses caused by your safe-breaking operations. Am I bringing an unjust indictment against you, pardner?"

A flicker of a smile was discernible somewhere in the tangle of beard that hid the lineaments of the prisoner's face.

"If I inventoried the contents of this bundle," continued Lowell, "I'd find a pretty complete outfit of the tools that keep the safe companies working overtime on replacements, wouldn't I?"

The prisoner nodded.

"There's no use of my dodgin', judge," he said. "The tools are there—all of 'em. But I'm through with the game. All I want now is enough of a stake to get me back home to Omaha, where the family is. That's why I was footin' it acrost this Injun country—takin' a short cut to a railroad where I wouldn't be watched for."

"I'll consider your case awhile," remarked Lowell after a moment's thought. "Perhaps we can speed you on your way to Omaha and the family."

The prisoner was taken back to the agency jail leaving his bundle on Lowell's desk. About midnight Lowell took the bundle and, going to the jail, roused the policeman who was on guard and was admitted to the prisoner's cell.

"Look here, Red," said Lowell. "Your name is Red, isn't it?"

"Red Egan."

"Well, Red Egan, did you ever hear of Jimmy Valentine?"

The prisoner scratched his head while he puffed at a welcome cigarette.

"No? Well, Red, this Jimmy Valentine was in the business you're quitting, and he opened a safe in a good cause. I want you to do the same for me. If you can do a neat job, with no noise, I'll see that you get across the reservation all right, with stake enough to get you to Omaha."

"You're on, judge! I'd crack one more for a good scout like you any day."

Three quarters of an hour later Red Egan was working professionally upon the safe in Bill Talpers's store. The door to Talpers's sleeping-room was not far away, but it was closed, and the trader was a thorough sleeper, so the cracksman might have been conducting operations a mile distant, so far as interruption from Bill was concerned.

As he worked, Red Egan told whispered stories to a companion—stories which related to barriers burned, pried, and blown away.

"I don't mind how close they sleep to their junk," observed Red, as he rested momentarily from his labors. "Unless a man's got insomnier and insists on makin' his bed on top of his safe, he ain't got a chance to make his iron doors stay shut if one of the real good 'uns takes a notion to make 'em fly apart. There she goes!" he added a moment later, as the safe door swung open.

"All right, Red," came the whispered reply, "but remember that I get whatever money's in sight, just for appearances' sake, though it's letters and such things I'm really after."

"It goes as you say, boss, and I hope you get what you want. There goes that inside door."

In the light of a flash-lamp Lowell saw a letter and a roll of bills. He took both, while Red Egan, his work done, packed up the kit of tools.

Lowell had recognized Helen's handwriting on the envelope, and knew he had found what he wanted.

"You've earned that trip to Omaha, Red," said Lowell, after they had gone back to their horses which had been standing in a cottonwood grove near by. "When we get back to the agency I'll put you in my car and drive you far enough by daybreak so that you can catch a train at noon."

"You're a square guy, judge, but if that's the letter you've been wantin' to get, why don't you read it? Or maybe you know what's in it without readin' it."

"No, I don't know what's in it, and I don't want to read it, Red."

Red's amazed whistle cut through the night silence.

"Well, if that ain't the limit! Havin' a safe-crackin' job done for a letter that you ain't ever seen and don't want to see the inside of!"

"It's all right, Red. Don't worry about it, because you've earned your money twice over to-night. Don't look on your last job as a failure, by any means."

A few hours later the Indian agent, not looking like a man who had been up all night, halted his car at Talpers's store, after he had received an excited hail from Andy Wolters.

"You're jest in time!" exclaimed Andy. "Bill Talpers's safe has been cracked and Bill is jest now tryin' to figger the damage. He says he's lost a roll of money and some other things."

Lowell found Talpers going excitedly through the contents of his broken safe. It was not the first time the trader had pawed over the papers. Nor were the oaths that fell on Lowell's ears the first that the trader had uttered since the discovery that he had been robbed as he slept.

It was plain enough that Talpers was suffering from a deeper shock than could come through any mere loss of money. Not even when Lowell contrived to drop the roll of bills, where the trader's clerk picked it up with a whoop of glee, did Talpers's expression change. His oaths were those of a man distraught, and the contumely he heaped upon Sheriff Tom Redmond moved that official to a spirited defense.

"I can't see why you hold me responsible for a safe that you've been keeping within earshot all these years," retorted Tom, in answer to Talpers's sneers about the lack of protection afforded the county's business men. "If you can't hear a yeggman working right next to your sleeping-quarters, how do you expect me to hear him, 'way over to White Lodge? I'll leave it to Lowell here if your complaint is reasonable. I'll do the best I can to get this man, but it looks to me as if he's made a clean getaway. What sort of papers was it you said you lost, Bill?"

"I didn't say."

"Well, then, I'm asking you. Was they long or short, rolled or flat, or tied with pink ribbon?"

"Never mind!" roared Talpers. "You round up this burglar and let me go through him. I'll get what's mine, all right."

Redmond made a gesture of despair. A man who had been robbed and had recovered his money, and was so keen after papers that he wouldn't or couldn't describe, was past all fooling with. The sheriff rode off, grumbling, without even questioning Lowell to ascertain if the Indian police had seen any suspicious characters on the reservation.

Bill Talpers's mental convolutions following the robbery reminded Lowell of the writhing of a wounded snake. Bill's fear was that the letter would be picked up and sent back to the girl at the Greek Letter Ranch. Suspicion of a plot in the affair did not enter his head. To him it was just a sinister stroke of misfortune—one of the chance buffets of fate. One tramp burglar out of the many pursuing that vocation had happened upon the Talpers establishment at a time when its proprietor was in an unusually sound sleep. Bill gave himself over to thoughts of the various forms of punishment he would inflict upon the wandering yeggman in case a capture were effected—thoughts which came to naught, as Red Egan had been given so generous a start toward his Omaha goal that he never was headed.

As the days went past and the letter was not discovered, Bill began to gather hope. Perhaps the burglar, thinking the letter of no value, had destroyed it, in natural disgust at finding that he had dropped the money which undoubtedly was the real object of his safe-breaking.

If Talpers had known what had really happened to the letter, all his self-comfortings would have vanished. Lowell had lost no time in taking the missive to Helen. He had found affairs at the Greek Letter Ranch apparently unchanged. Wong was at work in the kitchen. Two Indians, who had been hired to harvest the hay, which was the only crop on the ranch, were busy in a near-by field. Helen, looking charming in a house dress of blue, with white collar and cuffs, was feeding a tame magpie when Lowell drove into the yard.

"Moving picture entitled 'The Metamorphosis of Miss Tatters,'" said Lowell, amusedly surveying her.

"The scratches still survive, but the riding-suit will take a lot of mending," said Helen, showing her scratched hands and wrists.

"Well, if this very becoming costume has a pocket, here's something to put in it," remarked Lowell, handing her the letter.

Helen's smile was succeeded by a startled, anxious look, as she glanced at the envelope and then at Lowell.

"No need for worry," Lowell assured her. "Nobody has read that letter since it passed out of the possession of our esteemed postmaster, Bill Talpers, sometime after one o'clock this morning."

"But how did he come to give it up?" asked Helen, her voice wavering.

"He did not do so willingly. It might be said he did not give it up knowingly. As a matter of fact, our friend Talpers had no idea he had lost his precious possession until it had been gone several hours."

"But how—"

"'How' is a word to be flung at Red Egan, knight of the steel drill and the nitro bottle and other what-nots of up-to-date burglary," said Lowell. "Though I saw the thing done, I can't tell you how. I only hope it clears matters for you."

"It does in a way. I cannot tell you how grateful I am," said Helen, her trembling hands tightly clutching the letter.

"Only in a way? I am sorry it does not do more."

"But it's a very important way, I assure you!" exclaimed Helen. "It eliminates this man—this Talpers—as a personal menace. But when you are so eager to get every thread of evidence, how is it that you can give this letter to me, unread? You must feel sure it has some bearing on the awful thing—the tragedy that took place back there on the hill."

"That is where faith rises superior to a very human desire to look into the details of mystery," said Lowell. "If I were a real detective, or spy, as you characterized me, I would have read that letter at the first opportunity. But I knew that my reading it would cause you grave personal concern. I have faith in you to the extent that I believe you would do nothing to bring injustice upon others. Consequently, from now on I will proceed to forget that this letter ever existed."

"You may regret that you have acted in this generous manner," said the girl. "What if you find that all your faith has been misplaced—that I am not worthy of the trust—"

"Really, there is nothing to be gained by saying such things," interposed Lowell. "As I told you, I am forgetting that the letter ever existed."

"Do you know," she said, "I wish this letter could have come back to me from any one but you?"

"Why?"

"Because, coming as it has, I am more or less constrained to act as fairly as you believe I shall act."

"You might give it back to Talpers and start in on any sort of a deal you chose."

"Impossible! For fear Talpers may get it, here is what I shall do to the letter."

Here Helen tore it in small pieces and tossed them high in the air, the breeze carrying them about the yard like snow.

"In which event," laughed Lowell, "it seems that I win, and my faith in you is to be justified."

"I wish I could assure you of as much," answered Helen sadly. "But if it happens that your trust is not justified, I hope you will not think too harshly of me."

"Harshly!" exclaimed Lowell. "Harshly! Why, if you practiced revolver shooting on me an hour before breakfast every morning, or if you used me for a doormat here at the Greek Letter Ranch, I couldn't think anything but lovingly of you."

"Oh!" cried Helen, clapping her hands over her ears and running up the porch steps, as Lowell turned to his automobile. "You've almost undone all the good you've accomplished to-day."

"Thanks for that word 'almost,'" laughed Lowell.

"Then I'll make it 'quite,'" flung Helen, but her words were lost in the shifting of gears as Lowell started back to the agency.

That night Helen dreamed that Bill Talpers, on hands and knees, was moving like a misshapen shadow about the yard in the moonlight picking up the letter which she had torn to pieces.

CHAPTER XIII

Sheriff Tom Redmond sat in Lowell's office at the agency, staring grimly across at the little park, where the down from the cottonwood trees clung to the grass like snow. The sheriff had just brought himself to a virtual admission that he had been in the wrong.

"I was going to say," remarked Tom, "that, in case you catch Jim McFann, perhaps the best thing would be for you to sort o' close-herd him at the agency jail here until time for trial."

Lowell looked at the sheriff inquiringly.

"I'll admit that I've been sort of clamoring for you to let me bring a big posse over here and round up McFann in a hurry. Well, I don't believe that scheme would work."

"I'm glad we agree on that point."

"You've been taking the ground that unless we brought a lot of men over, we couldn't do any better than the Injun police in the matter of catching this half-breed. Also you've said that if we *did* bring a small army of cattlemen, it would only be a lynching party, and Jim McFann'd never live to reach the jail at White Lodge."

"I don't think anything could stop a lynching."

"Well, I believe you're right. The boys have been riding me, stronger and stronger, to get up a posse and come over here. In fact, they got so strong that I suspected they had something up their sleeves. When I sort o' backed up on the proposition, a lot of them began pulling wires at Washington, so's to make you get orders that'd let us come on the reservation and get both of these men."

"I know it," said Lowell, "but they've found they can't make any headway, even with their own Congressmen, because Judge Garford's stand is too well known. He's let everybody know that he's against anything that may bring about a lynching. So far as the Department is concerned, I've put matters squarely up to it and have been advised to use my own judgment."

"Well, I never seen people so wrought up, and I'm free to admit now that if Jim McFann hadn't broke jail he'd have been lynched on the very day that he made his getaway. The only question is—do you think you can get him before the trial, and are you sure the Injun'll come in?"

"I'm not sure of anything, of course," replied Lowell, "but I've staked everything on Fire Bear making good his word. If he doesn't, I'm ready to quit the country. McFann's a different proposition. He has been too clever for the police, but I have rather hesitated about having Plenty Buffalo risk the lives of his men, because I have had a feeling that McFann might be reached in a different way. I'm sure he's been getting supplies from the man who has been using him in bootlegging operations."

"You mean Talpers?"

"Yes. If McFann is mixed up in anything, from bootlegging to bigger crimes, he is only a tool. He can be a dangerous tool—that's admitted—but I'd like to gather in the fellow who does the planning."

"By golly! I wish I had you working with me on this murder case," said Redmond, in a burst of confidence. "I'll admit I never had anything stump me the way this case has. I'm bringing up against a blank wall at every turn."

"Haven't you found out anything new about Sargent?"

"Not a thing worth while. He lived alone—had lots of money that he made by inventing mining machinery."

"Any relatives?"

"None that we can find out about."

"Have you learned anything through his bank?"

"He had plenty of money on deposit; that's all."

"Did he have any lawyers?"

"Not that we've heard from."

"Does any one know why he came on this trip?"

"No; but he was in the habit of making long jaunts alone through the West."

"What sort of a home did he have?"

"A big house in the suburbs. Lived there alone with two servants. They haven't been able to tell a thing about him that's worth a cuss."

"Would anything about his home indicate what sort of a man he was?"

"The detectives wrote something about his having a lot of Indian things—Navajo blankets and such."

"Indians may have been his hobby. Perhaps he intended to visit this reservation."

"If that was so, why should he drive through the agency at night and be killed going away from the reservation? No, he was going somewhere in a hurry or he wouldn't have traveled at night."

"But automobile tourists sometimes travel that way."

"Not in this part of the country. In the Southwest, perhaps, to avoid the heat of the day."

"Well, what do you think about it all, Tom?"

"That this feller was a pilgrim, going somewhere in a hurry. He was held up by some of your young bucks who were off the reservation and feeling a little too full of life for their own good. A touch of bootleg whiskey might have set them going. Mebbe that's where Jim McFann came in. They might have killed the man when he resisted. The staking-out was probably an afterthought—a piece of Injun or half-breed devilment."

"How about the sawed-off shotgun? I doubt if there's one on the reservation."

"Probably that was Sargent's own weapon. He had traveled in the West a good many years. Mebbe he had used sawed-off shotguns as an express messenger or something of the sort in early days. It's a fact that there ain't any handier weapon of *dee*fense than a sawed-off shotgun, no matter what kind of a wheeled outfit you're traveling in."

"It's all reasonable enough, Tom," said Lowell reflectively. "It may work out just as you have figured, but frankly I don't believe the Indians and McFann are in it quite as far as you think."

"Well, if they didn't do it, who could have? You've been over the ground more than any one else. Have you found anything to hang a whisper of suspicion on?"

Lowell shook his head.

"Nothing to talk about, but there are some things, indefinite enough, perhaps, that make me hesitate about believing the Indians to be guilty."

"How about McFann? He's got the nerve, all right."

"Yes, McFann would kill if it came to a showdown. There's enough Indian in him, too, to explain the staking-down."

"He admits he was on the scene of the murder."

"Yes, and his admission strengthens me in the belief that he's telling the truth, or at least that he had no part in the actual killing. If he were guilty, he'd deny being within miles of the spot."

"Mebbe you're right," said the sheriff, rising and turning his hat in his hand and methodically prodding new and geometrically perfect indentations in its high crown, "but you've got a strong popular opinion to buck. Most people believe them Injuns and the breed have a guilty knowledge of the murder."

"When you get twelve men in the jury box saying the same thing," replied Lowell, "that's going to settle it. But until then I'm considering the case open."

Jim McFann's camp was in the loneliest of many lonely draws in the sage-gray uplands where the foothills and plains meet. It was not a camp that would appeal to the luxury-loving. In fact, one might almost fall over it in the brush before knowing that a camp was there. A "tarp" bed was spread on the hard, sun-cracked soil. A saddle was near by. There was a frying-pan or two at the edge of a dead fire. A pack-animal and saddle horse stood disconsolately in the greasewood, getting what slender grazing was available, but not being allowed to wander far. It was the camp of one who "traveled light" and was ready to go at an instant's notice.

So well hidden was the half-breed that, in spite of explicit directions that had been given by Bill Talpers, Andy Wolters had a difficult time in finding the camp. Talpers had sent Andy as his emissary, bearing grub and tobacco and a bottle of whiskey to the half-breed. Andy had turned and twisted most of the morning in the monotony of sage. Song had died upon his lips as the sun had beaten upon him with all its unclouded vigor.

Andy did not know it, but for an hour he had been under the scrutiny of the half-breed, who had been quick to descry the horseman moving through the brush. McFann had been expecting Talpers, and he was none too pleased to find that the trader had sent the gossiping cowpuncher in his stead. Andy, being one of those ingenuous souls who never can catch the undercurrents of life, rattled on, all unconscious of the effect of light words, lightly flung.

"You dig the grub and other stuff out o' that pack," said Andy, "while I hunt an inch or two of shade and cool my brow. When it comes to makin' a success of hidin' out in the brush, you can beat one of them renegade steers that we miss every round-up. I guess you ain't heard about the robbery that's happened in our metropolis of Talpersville, have you?"

The half-breed grunted a negative.

"Of course not, seein' as you ain't gettin' the daily paper out here. Well, an expert safe-buster rode Bill Talpers's iron treasure-chest to a frazzle the other night. Took valuable papers that Bill's all fussed up about, but dropped a wad of bills, big enough to choke one of them prehistoric bronks that used to romp around in these hills."

McFann looked up scowlingly from his task of estimating the amount of grub that had been sent.

"Seems to me," went on Andy, "that if I got back my money, I wouldn't give a durn about papers—not unless they was papers that established my rights as the long-lost heir of some feller with about twenty million dollars. That roll had a thousand-dollar bill wrapped around the outside."

The half-breed straightened up.

"How do you know there was a thousand-dollar bill in that roll?" he demanded, with an intensity that surprised the cowboy.

"Bill told me so himself. He had took a few snifters, and was feelin' melancholy over them papers, and I tried to cheer him up by tellin' him jest what I've told you, that as long as I had my roll back, I wouldn't care about all the hen-tracks that spoiled nice white paper. He chirked up a bit at that, and got confidential and told me about this thousand-dollar bill. They say it ain't the only one he had. The story is that he sprung one on an Injun the other day in payment for a bunch o' steers. There must be lots more profit in prunes and shawls and the other things that Bill handles than most people have been thinkin', with thousand-dollar bills comin' so easy."

The half-breed was listening intently now. He had ceased his work about the camp, and was standing, with hands clenched and head thrust forward, eyeing Andy so narrowly that the cowboy paused in his narrative.

"What's the matter, Jim?" he asked; "Bill didn't take any of them thousand-dollar things from you, did he?"

"Mebbe not, and mebbe so," enigmatically answered the half-breed. "Go on and tell me the rest."

When he had completed his story of the robbery at Talpers's store, Andy tilted his enormous sombrero over his eyes, and, leaning back in the shade, fell asleep. The half-breed worked silently about the camp, occasionally going to a near-by knoll and looking about for some sign of life in the sagebrush. He made some biscuits and coffee and fried some bacon, after which he touched Andy none too gently with his moccasined foot and told the cowboy to sit up and eat something.

After one or two ineffectual efforts to start conversation, the visitor gave up in disgust. The meal was eaten in silence. Even the obtuse Andy sensed that something was wrong, and made no effort to rouse the half-breed, who ate grimly and immediately busied himself with the dish-washing as soon as the meal was over. Andy soon took his departure, the half-breed directing him to a route that would lessen the chances of his discovery by the Indian police.

After Andy had gone the half-breed turned his attention to the bottle which had been sent by Talpers. He visited the knoll occasionally, but nothing alive could be discerned in the great wastes of sage. When the shadows deepened and the chill of evening came down from the high altitudes of the near-by peaks, McFann staked out his ponies in better grazing ground. Then he built a small camp-fire, and, sitting cross-legged in the light, he smoked and drank, and meditated upon the perfidy of Bill Talpers.

McFann was astir at dawn, and there was determination in every move as he brought in the horses and began to break camp.

The half-breed owned a ranch which had come down to him from his Indian mother. Shrewdly suspecting that the police had ceased watching the ranch, Jim made his way homeward. His place was located in the bottom-land along a small creek. There was a shack on it, but no attempt at cultivation. As he looked the place over, Jim's thoughts became more bitter than ever. If he had farmed this land, the way the agent wanted him to, he could have been independent by now, but instead of that he had listened to Talpers's blandishments and now had been thrown down by his professed friend!

Jim took off his pack and threw his camping equipment inside the shack. Then he turned his pack-animal into the wild hay in the pasture he had fenced off in the creek bottom. He had some other live stock roaming around in the little valley—enough steers and horses to make a beginning toward a comfortable independence, if he had only had sense enough to start in that way. Also there was good soil on the upland. He could run a ditch from the creek to the nearest mesa, where the land was red and sandy and would raise anything. The reservation agriculturist had been along and had shown him just how the trick could be done, but Bill Talpers's bootlegging schemes looked a lot better then!

The half-breed slammed his shack door shut and rode away with his greasy hat-brim pulled well over his eyes. He paid little attention to the demands he was making on horseflesh, and he rode openly across the country. If the Indian police saw him, he could outdistance them. The thing that he had set out to do could be done quickly. After that, nothing mattered much.

Skirting the ridge on which Helen and Lowell had stood, Jim made a détour as he approached the reservation line and avoided the Greek Letter Ranch. He swung into the road well above the ranch, and, breasting the hill where the murder had taken place on the Dollar Sign, he galloped down the slope toward Talpers's store.

The trader was alone in his store when the half-breed entered. Talpers had seen McFann coming, some distance down the road. Something in the half-breed's bearing in the saddle, or perhaps it was some inner stir of guilty fear, made Talpers half-draw his revolver. Then he thrust it back into its holster, and, swinging around in his chair, awaited his partner's arrival. He even attempted a jaunty greeting.

"Hello, Jim," he called, as the half-breed's lithe figure swung in through the outer doorway; "ain't you even a little afraid of the Injun police?"

McFann did not answer, but flung open the door into Bill's sanctum. It was no unusual thing for the men to confer there, and two or three Indians on the front porch did not even turn their heads to see what was going on inside. Talpers's clerk was out and Andy Wolters had just departed, after reporting to the trader that the half-breed had seemed "plumb uneasy out there in the brush." Andy had not told Bill the cause of McFann's uneasiness, but on that point the trader was soon to be enlightened.

"Bill," said the half-breed purringly, "I hear you've been having your safe cracked."

Something in the half-breed's voice made the trader wish he had not shoved back that revolver. It would not do to reach for it now. McFann's hands were empty, but he was lightning in getting them to his guns.

The trader's lips seemed more than usually dry and cracked. His voice wheezed at the first word, as he answered.

"Yes, Jim, I was robbed," he said. Then he added, propitiatingly: "But I've got a new safe. Ain't she a beauty?"

"She sure is," replied McFann, though he did not take his eyes off Talpers. "Got your name on, and everything. Let's open her up, and see what a real safe looks like inside."

Talpers turned without question and began fumbling at the combination. His hands trembled, and once he dropped them at his side. As he did so McFann's hands moved almost imperceptibly. Their movement was toward the half-breed's hips, and Talpers brought his own hands quickly back to the combination. The tumblers fell, and the trader swung the door open.

"Purtier 'n a new pair of boots," approved the half-breed, as a brave array of books and inner drawers came in view. "Now them inside boxes. The one with the thousand-dollar bill in it."

"Why, what's gittin' into you, Jim?" almost whined Talpers. "You know I ain't got any thousand-dollar bill."

"Don't lie to me," snapped the half-breed, a harsh note coming into his voice. "You've made your talk about a thousand-dollar bill. I want to see it—that's all."

Slowly Talpers unlocked the inner strong box and took therefrom a roll of money.

"There it is," he said, handing it to McFann. A thousand-dollar bill was on the outside of the roll.

"I ain't going to ask where you got that," said McFann steadily, "because you'd lie to me. But I know. You took it from that man on the hill. You told me you'd jest found him there when I come on you prowling around his body. You said you didn't take anything from him, and I was fool enough to believe you. But you didn't get these thousand-dollar bills anywhere else. You double-crossed me, and if things got too warm for you, you was going to saw everything off on me. Easy enough when I was hiding out there in the sagebrush, living on what you wanted to send out to me. I've done all this bootlegging work for you, and I covered up for you in court, about this murder, all because I thought you was on the square. And all the time you had took your pickings from this man on the hill and had fooled me into thinking you didn't find a thing on him. Here's the money, Bill. I wouldn't take it away from you. Lock it in your safe again—if you can!"

The half-breed flung the roll of bills in Talpers's face. The trader, made desperate by fear, flung himself toward McFann. If he could pinion the half-breed's arms to his side, there could be but one outcome to the struggle that had been launched. The trader's great weight and grizzly-like strength would be too much for the wiry half-breed to overcome. But McFann slipped easily away from Talpers's clutching hands. The trader brought up against the mailing desk with a crash that shook the entire building. The heat of combat warmed his chilled veins. Courage returned to him with a rush. He roared oaths as he righted himself and dragged his revolver from the holster on his hip.

Before the trader's gun could be brought to a shooting level, paralysis seemed to seize his arm. Fire seared his side and unbearable pain radiated therefrom. Only the fighting man's instinct kept him on his feet. His knees sagged and his arm drooped slowly, despite his desperate endeavors to raise that blue-steel weapon to its target. He saw the half-breed, smiling and defiant, not three paces away, but seemingly in another world. There was a revolver in McFann's hand, and faint tendrils of smoke came from the weapon.

Grimly setting his jaws and with his lips parted in a mirthless grin, Talpers crossed his left hand to his right. With both hands he tried to raise the revolver, but it only sank lower. His knees gave way and he slid to the floor, his back to his new safe and his swarthy skin showing a pale yellow behind his sparse, curling black beard.

"Put the money away, Bill, put it away, quick," said McFann's mocking voice. "There it is, under your knee. You sold out your pardner for it—now hide it in your new safe!"

Talpers's cracked lips formed no reply, but his little black eyes glowed balefully behind their dark, lowering brows.

"You're good at shooting down harmless Indians, Bill," jeered McFann, "but you're too slow in a real fight. Any word you want to send to the Indian agent? I'm going to tell him I believe you did the murder on the Dollar Sign road."

A last flare of rage caused Talpers to straighten up. Then the paralysis came again, stronger than before. The revolver slipped from the trader's grasp, and his head sank forward until his chin rested on his broad chest.

McFann looked contemptuously at the great figure, helpless in death. Then he lighted a cigarette, and, laughing at the terror of the Indians, who had been peeping in the window at the last of the tragedy, the half-breed walked out of the store, and, mounting his horse, rode to the agency and gave himself up to Lowell.

CHAPTER XIV

Lowell consulted with Judge Garford and Sheriff Tom Redmond, and it was decided to keep Jim McFann in jail at the agency until time for his trial for complicity in the first murder on the Dollar Sign road.

Sheriff Redmond admitted that, owing to the uncertainty of public sentiment, he could not guarantee the half-breed's safety if McFann were lodged in the county jail. Consequently the slayer of Bill Talpers remained in jail at the agency, under a strong guard of Indian police, supplemented by trustworthy deputies sent over by Redmond.

The killing of Talpers was the excuse for another series of attacks on Lowell by the White Lodge paper. Said the editor:

> The murder of our esteemed neighbor, William Talpers, by James McFann, a half-breed, is another evidence of the necessity of opening the reservation to white settlement.
>
> This second murder on the Dollar Sign road is not a mystery. Its perpetrator was seen at this bloody work. Furthermore, he is understood to have coolly confessed his crime. But, like the first murder, which is still shrouded in mystery, this was a crime which found its inception on the Indian reservation. Are white residents adjacent to the reservation to have their lives snuffed out at the pleasure of Government wards and reservation offscourings in general? Has not the time come when the broad acres of the Indian reservation, which the redskins are doing little with, should be thrown open to the plough of the white man?

"'Plough of the white man' is good," cynically observed Ed Rogers, after calling Lowell's attention to the article. "If those cattlemen ever get the reservation opened, they'll keep the nesters out for the next forty years, if they have to kill a homesteader for every hundred and sixty acres. So far as Bill Talpers's killing is concerned, I can't see but what it is looked upon as a good thing for the peace of the community."

It seemed to be a fact that Jim McFann's act had appealed irresistibly to a large element. Youthful cowpunchers rode for miles and waited about the agency for a glimpse of the gun-fighter who had slain the redoubtable Bill Talpers in such a manner. None of them could get near the jail, but they stood in picturesque groups about the agency, listening to the talk of Andy Wolters and others who had been on more or less intimate terms with the principals in the affair.

"And there was me a-snoozin' in that breed's camp the very day before he done this shootin'," said Andy to an appreciative circle. "He must have had this thing stewin' in his head at the time. It's a wonder he didn't throw down on me, jest for a little target practice. But I guess he figgered he didn't need no practice to get Bill Talpers, and judgin' from the way things worked out, his figgerin' was right. Some artist with the little smoke machine, that boy, 'cause Bill Talpers wasn't no slouch at shootin'! I remember seein' Bill shoot the head off a rattlesnake at the side of the road, jest casual-like, and when it come to producin' the hardware he was some quick for a big man. He more than met his match this time, old Bill did. And, by gosh! you can bet that nobody after this ever sends me out to any dry camps in the brush to take supplies to any gunman who may be hid out there. Next time I might snooze and never wake up."

All was not adulation for Jim McFann. Because of the Indian strain in his blood a minor undercurrent of prejudice had set in against him, more particularly among the white settlers and the cattlemen who were casting covetous eyes on reservation lands. While McFann was not strictly a ward of the Government, he had land on the reservation. His lot was cast with the Indians, chiefly because he found few white men who would associate with him on account of his Indian blood. Talpers was not loved, but the killing of any white man by some one of Indian ancestry was something to fan resentment without regard to facts. Bets were made that McFann would not live to be tried on the second homicide charge against him, many holding the opinion that he would be hanged, with Fire Bear, for the first murder. Also wagers were freely made that Fire Bear would not be produced in court by the Indian agent, and that it would be necessary to send a force of officers to get the accused Indian.

Lowell apparently paid no attention to the rumors that were flying about. A mass of reservation detail had accumulated, and he worked hard to get it out of the way before the trial. He had made changes in the boarding-school system, and had established an experimental farm at the agency. He had supervised the purchase of livestock for the improvement of the tribal flocks and herds. In addition there had been the personal demands that shower incessantly upon every Indian agent who is interested in his work.

Reports from the reservation agriculturists, whose work was to help the Indians along farming lines, were not encouraging. Drought was continuing without abatement.

"The last rain fell the day before the murder on the Dollar Sign road," said Rogers. "Remember how we splashed through mud the day we ran out there and found that man staked down on the prairie?"

"And now the Indians are saying that the continued drought is due to Fire Bear's medicine," observed Lowell. "Even some of the more conservative Indians believe there is no use trying to raise crops until the charge against Fire Bear is dismissed and the evil spell is lifted."

In spite of the details of reservation management that crowded upon him, Lowell found time for occasional visits to the Greek Letter Ranch to see Helen Ervin. He told her the details of the Talpers shooting, so far as he knew them.

"There isn't much that I can tell about the cause of the shooting," said Lowell, in answer to one of her questions. "I could have had all the details, but I cautioned Jim McFann to say nothing in advance of his trial. But from what I have gathered here and there, Jim and Talpers fell out over money matters. A thousand-dollar bill was found on the floor under Talpers's body. It had evidently been taken from the safe, and might have been what they fought over."

Helen nodded in comprehension of the whole affair, though she did not tell Lowell that he had made it clear to her. She guessed that in some way Jim McFann had come into possession of the facts of his partner's perfidy. She wondered how the half-breed had found out that Talpers had taken money from the murdered man and had not divided. She had held that knowledge over Talpers's head as a club. She could see that he feared McFann, and she wondered if, in his last moments, Talpers had wrongfully blamed her for giving the half-breed the information which turned him into a slayer.

"Anyway, it doesn't make much difference what the fight was over," declared Lowell. "Talpers had been playing a double game for a long time.

He tried just once too often to cheat his partner—something dangerous when that partner is a fiery-tempered half-breed."

"Is this shooting of Talpers going to have any effect on McFann's trial for the other murder?" asked Helen.

"It may inflame popular sentiment against both men still further—something that never seems to be difficult where Indians are concerned."

Lowell tried in vain to lead the talk away from the trial.

"Look here," he exclaimed finally, "you're worrying yourself unnecessarily over this! I don't believe you're getting much of any sleep, and I'll bet Wong will testify that you are eating very little. You mustn't let matters weigh on your mind so. Talpers is gone, and you have the letter that was in his safe and that he used as a means of worrying you. Your stepfather is getting better right along—so much so that you can leave here at any time. Pretty soon you'll have this place of tragedy off your mind and you'll forget all about the Indian reservation and everything it contains. But until that time comes, I prescribe an automobile ride for you every day. Some of the roads around here will make it certain that you will be well shaken before the prescription is taken."

Lowell regretted his light words as soon as he had uttered them.

"This trial is my whole life," declared the girl solemnly. "If those men are convicted, there can never be another day of happiness for me!"

On the morning set for the opening of the trial, Lowell left his automobile in front of his residence while he ate breakfast. To all appearances there was nothing unusual about this breakfast. It was served at the customary time and in the customary way. Apparently the young Indian agent was interested only in the meal and in some letters which had been sent over from the office, but finally he looked up and smiled at the uneasiness of his housekeeper, who had cast frequent glances out of the window.

"What is it, Mrs. Ruel?" asked Lowell.

"The Indian—Fire Bear. Has he come?"

"Oh, that's what's worrying you, is it? Well, don't let it do so any more. He will be here all right."

Mrs. Ruel looked doubtful as she trotted to the kitchen. Returning, she stood in the window, a steaming coffee-pot in her hands.

"Tell me what you see, Sister Annie," said Lowell smilingly.

"Nawthin' but the kids assemblin' for school. There's old Pete, the blacksmith, purtendin' to be lookin' your machine over, when he's just come to rubber the way I am, f'r that red divvle. They're afraid, most of the agency folks, that Fire Bear won't show up. I wouldn't take an Injun's word f'r annythin' myself—me that lost an uncle in the Fetterman massacree. You're too good to 'em, Mister Lowell. You should have yanked this Fire Bear here in handcuffs—him and McFann together."

"Your coffee is fine—and I'll be obliged if you'll pour me some—but your philosophy is that of the dark ages, Mrs. Ruel. Thanks. Now tell me what traveler approaches on the king's highway."

Mrs. Ruel trotted to the window, with the coffee-pot still in her hands.

"It's some one of them educated loafers that's always hangin' around the trader's store. I c'n tell by the hang of the mail-order suit. No, it ain't! He's climbin' off his pony, and now he's jumped into the back of your automobile, and is settin' there, bold as brass, smokin' a cigarette. It's Fire Bear himself!"

"I thought so," observed Lowell. "Now another cup of coffee, please, and a little more of that toast, and we'll be off to the trial."

Mrs. Ruel returned to the kitchen, declaring that it really didn't prove anything in general, because no other agent could make them redskins do the things that Mister Lowell hypnotized 'em into doin'.

Lowell finished his breakfast and climbed into his automobile, after a few words with Fire Bear. The young Indian had started the day before from his camp in the rocks. He had traveled alone, and had not rested until he reached the agency. Lowell knew there would be much dancing in the Indian camp until the trial was over.

Driving to the agency jail, Lowell had McFann brought out. The half-breed, unmanacled and without a guard, sat beside Fire Bear in the back seat. Lowell decided to take no policemen from the reservation. He was certain that Fire Bear and McFann would not try to escape from him. The presence of Indian policemen might serve only to fan the very uncertain public sentiment into disastrous flames.

White Lodge was crowded with cattlemen and homesteaders and their families, who had come to attend the trial. A public holiday was made of the occasion, and White Lodge had not seen such a crowd since the annual bronco-busting carnival.

As he drove through the streets, Lowell was conscious of a change in public feeling. The prisoners in the automobile were eyed curiously, but without hatred. In fact, Jim McFann's killing of Talpers, which had been given all sorts of dramatic renditions at camp-fires and firesides, had raised that worthy to the rank of hero in the eyes of the majority. Also the coming of Fire Bear, as he had promised, sent up the Indian's stock. As Lowell took his men to the court-room he saw bets paid over by men who had wagered that Fire Bear would not keep his word and that he would have to be brought to the court-room by force.

The court-house yard could not hold the overflow of spectators from the court-room. The crowd was orderly, though there was a tremendous craning of necks when the prisoners were brought in, to see the man who had killed so redoubtable a gunman as Bill Talpers. Getting a jury was merely a matter of form, as no challenges were made. The trial opened with Fire Bear on the stand.

The young Indian added nothing to the testimony he had given at his preliminary hearing. He told, briefly, how he and his followers had found the body beside the Dollar Sign road. The prosecuting attorney was quick to sense a difference in the way the Indian's story was received. When he had first told it, disbelief was evident. Today it seemed to be impressing crowd and jury as the truth.

The same sentiment seemed to be even more pronounced when Jim McFann took the stand, after Fire Bear's brief testimony was concluded without cross-examination. Audience and jury sat erect. Word was passed out to the crowd that the half-breed was testifying. In the court-room there was such a stir that the bailiff was forced to rap for order.

The prosecuting attorney, seeing the case slipping away from him, was moved to frantic denunciations. He challenged McFann's every statement.

"You claim that you had lost your lariat and were looking for it. Also that you came upon this dead body, with your rope used to fasten the murdered man to stakes that had been driven into the prairie?" sneered the attorney.

"Yes;" said McFann.

"And you claim that you were frightened away by the arrival of Fire Bear and his Indians before you had a chance to remove the rope?"

"Yes; but I want to add something to that statement," said the half-breed.

"All right—what is it?"

"There was another man by the body when I came there looking for my rope."

"Who was that man?"

"Talpers."

A thrill ran through the court-room as the half-breed went on and described how he had found the trader stooping over the murdered man, and how Talpers had shown him a watch which he had taken from the victim, but claimed that was all the valuables that had been found. Also he described how Talpers had prevailed upon him to keep the trader's presence a secret, which McFann had done in his previous testimony.

"Why do you come in with this story, at this late day?" asked the attorney.

"Because Talpers was lying to me all the time. He had taken money from that man—some of it in thousand-dollar bills. I did not care for the money. It was just that this man had lied to me, after I had done all his bootlegging work. He was playing safe at my expense. If it had been found that the dead man was robbed, he was ready to lay the blame on me. When I heard of the money he had hidden, I knew the game he had played. I walked in on him, and made him take the dead man's money from his safe. I threw the money in his face and dared him to fight. When he tried to shoot me, I killed him. It was better that he should die. I don't care what you do with me, but how are you going to hang Fire Bear or hang me for being near that body, *when Bill Talpers was there first*?"

Jim McFann's testimony remained unshaken. Cast doubt upon it as he would, the prosecuting attorney saw that the half-breed's new testimony had given an entirely new direction to the trial. He ceased trying to stem the tide and let the case go to the jury.

The crowd filed out, but waited around the court-house for the verdict. The irrepressible cowpunchers, who had a habit of laying wagers on anything and everything, made bets as to the number of minutes the jury would be out.

"Whichever way it goes, it'll be over in a hurry," said Tom Redmond to Lowell, "but hanged if I don't believe your men are as good as free this minute. Talpers's friends have been trying to stir up a lot of sentiment against Jim McFann, but it has worked the other way. The hull county seems to think right now that McFann done the right sort of a job, and that Talpers was not only a bootlegger, but was not above murder, and was the man who committed that crime on the Dollar Sign road. Of course, if Talpers done it, Fire Bear couldn't have. Furthermore, this young Injun has made an awful hit by givin' himself up for trial the way he has. To tell you the truth, I didn't think he'd show up."

Lowell escaped as soon as he could from the excited sheriff and sought Helen Ervin, whom he had seen in the court-room.

"I'm sorry I couldn't come to get you, on account of having to bring in the prisoners," said Lowell, "but I imagine this is the last ride to White Lodge you will have to take. The jury is going to decide quickly—or such is the general feeling."

Lowell had hardly spoken when a shout from the crowd on the court-house steps announced to the others that the jury had come in.

Lowell and Helen found places in the court-room. Judge Garford had not left his chambers. As soon as the crowd had settled down, the foreman announced the verdict.

"Not guilty!" was the word that was passed to those outside the building. There was a slight ripple of applause in the court-room which the bailiff's gavel checked. Lowell could not help but smile bitterly as he thought of the different sentiment at the close of the preliminary hearing, such a short time before. He wondered if the same thought had come to Judge Garford. But if the aged jurist had made any comparisons, they were not reflected in his benign features. A lifetime among scenes of turbulence, and watching justice gain steady ascendancy over frontier lawlessness, had made the judge indifferent to the manifestations of the moment.

"It's just as though we were a lot of jumping-jacks," thought Lowell, "and while we're doing all sorts of crazy things, the judge is looking far back behind the scenes studying the forces that are making us go. And he must be satisfied with what he sees or our illogical actions wouldn't worry him so little."

Fire Bear and McFann took the verdict with customary calm. The Indian was released from custody and took his place in Lowell's automobile. The half-breed was remanded to jail for trial for the Talpers slaying. Lowell, after saying good-bye to the half-breed, lost no time in starting for the agency. On the way he caught up with Helen, who was riding leisurely homeward. As he stopped the machine she reined up her horse beside him and extended her hand in congratulation.

"You're not the only one who is glad of the acquittal," she exclaimed. "I am glad—oh, I cannot tell you how much!"

Lowell noticed that her expression of girlishness had returned. The shadow which had fallen upon her seemed to have been lifted miraculously.

"Wasn't it strange the way things turned out?" she went on. "A little while ago every one seemed to believe these men were guilty, and now there's not a one who doesn't seem to think that Talpers did it."

"There's one who doesn't subscribe to the general belief," answered Lowell.

"What do you mean?"

Lowell was conscious that she was watching him narrowly.

"I mean that I don't believe Bill Talpers had anything to do with murdering that man on the Dollar Sign road!"

CHAPTER XV

"There's one thing sure in all cases of crime: If people would only depend more on Nature and less on themselves, they'd get results sooner."

Lowell and his chief clerk were finishing one of their regular evening discussions of the crime which most people were forgetting, but which still occupied the Indian agent's mind to the complete exclusion of all reservation business.

"What do you mean?" asked Rogers, from behind smoke clouds.

"Just the fact that, if we can only find it, Nature has tagged every crime in a way that makes it possible to get an answer."

"But there are lots of crimes in which no manifestation of Nature is possible."

"Not a one. What are finger-prints but manifestations of Nature? And yet for ages we couldn't see the sign that Nature hung out for us. No doubt we're just as obtuse about a lot of things that will be just as simple and just as plain when their meaning is finally driven home."

"But Nature hasn't given a hint about that Dollar Sign road crime. Yet it took place outdoors, right in Nature's haunts."

"You simply mean that we haven't been able to comprehend Nature's signals."

"But you've been over the ground a dozen times, haven't you?"

"Fifty times—but all that merely proves what I contend. If I go over that ground one hundred times, and don't find anything, what does it prove? Merely that I am ninety-nine times stupider than I should be. I should get the answer the first time over."

Rogers laughed.

"I prefer the most comfortable theory. I've settled down in the popular belief that Bill Talpers did the killing. Think how easy that makes it for me—and the chances are that I'm right at that."

"You are hopeless, Ed! But remember, if this thing goes unsolved it will only be because we haven't progressed beyond the first-reader stage in interpreting what Mother Nature has to teach us."

For several days following the acquittal of Fire Bear and McFann, Lowell had worked almost unceasingly in the hope of getting new evidence in the case which nearly everybody else seemed willing to forget. A similar persistency had marked Lowell's career as a newspaper reporter. He had turned up several sensations when rival newspaper men had abandoned certain cases as hopeless so far as new thrills were concerned.

Lowell had not exaggerated when he told Rogers he had gone over the scene of the murder fifty times. He had not gone into details with his clerk. Rogers would have been surprised to know that his chief had even blocked out the scene of the murder in squares like a checkerboard. Each one of these squares had been examined, slowly and painfully. The net result had been some loose change which undoubtedly had been dropped by Talpers in robbing the murdered man; an eagle feather, probably dropped from a *coup* stick which some one of Fire Bear's followers had borrowed from an elder; a flint arrowhead of great antiquity, and a belt buckle and some moccasin beads.

Far from being discouraged at the unsuccessful outcome of his checkerboarding plan, Lowell took his automobile, on the morning following his talk with Rogers, and again visited the scene of the crime.

For six weeks the hill had been bathed daily in sunshine. The drought, which the Indians had ascribed to evil spirits called down by Fire Bear, had continued unbroken. The mud-holes in the road, through which Lowell had plunged to the scene of the murder when he had first heard of the crime, had been churned to dust. Lowell noticed that an old buffalo wallow at the side of the road was still caked in irregular formations which resembled the markings of alligator hide. The first hot winds would cause these cakes of mud to disintegrate, but the weather had been calm, and they had remained just as they had dried.

As he glanced about him at the peaceful panorama, it occurred to the agent that perhaps too much attention had been centered upon the exact spot of the murder. Yet, it seemed reasonable enough to suppose, no murderer would possibly lie in wait for a victim in such an open spot. If the murder had been deliberately planned, as Lowell believed, and if the victim's approach were known, there could have been no waiting here on the part of the murderer.

Getting into his automobile, Lowell drove carefully up the hill, studying both sides of the road as he went. Several hundred yards from the scene of the murder, he found a clump of giant sagebrush and greasewood, close to the road. Lowell entered the clump and found that from its eastern side he could command a good view of the Dollar Sign road for miles. Here a man and horse might remain hidden until a traveler, coming up the hill, was almost within hailing distance. The brush had grown in a circle, leaving a considerable hollow which was devoid of vegetation. Examining this hollow closely, Lowell paused suddenly and uttered a low ejaculation. Then he walked slowly to his automobile and drove in the direction of the Greek Letter Ranch.

When he arrived at the ranch house Lowell was relieved to find that Helen was not at home. Wong, who opened the door a scant six inches, told him she had taken the white horse and gone for a ride.

"Well, tell Mister Willis Morgan I want to see him," said Lowell.

Wong was much alarmed. Mister Morgan could not be seen. The Chinese combination of words for "impossible" was marshaled in behalf of Wong's employer.

Lowell, putting his shoulder against the Greek letter brand which was burnt in the panel, pushed the door open and stepped into the room which served as a library.

"Now tell Mister Morgan I wish to see him, Wong," said the agent firmly.

The door to the adjoining room opened, and Lowell faced the questioning gaze of a gray-haired man who might have been anywhere from forty-five to sixty. One hand was in the pocket of a velvet smoking-jacket, and the other held a pipe. The man's eyes were dark and deeply set. They did not seem to Lowell to be the contemplative eyes of the scholar, but rather to belong to a man of decisive action—one whose interests might be in building bridges or tunnels, but whose activities were always concerned with material things. His face was lean and bronzed—the face of a man who lived much in the outdoors. His nose was aquiline, and his lips, though thin and firm, were not unkindly. In fact, here was a man who, in the class-room, might be given to quips with his students, rather than to sternness. Yet this was the man of whom it was said.... Lowell's face grew stern as the long list of indictments against Willis Morgan, recluse and "squaw professor," came to his mind.

The gray-haired man sat down at the table, and Lowell, in response to a wave of the hand that held the pipe, drew up opposite.

"You and I have been living pretty close together a long time," said Lowell bluntly, "and if we'd been a little more neighborly, this call might not be so difficult in some ways."

"My fault entirely." Again the hand waved—this time toward the ceiling-high shelves of books. "Library slavery makes a man selfish, I'll admit."

The voice was cold and hard. It was such a voice that had extended a mocking welcome to Helen Ervin when she had stood hesitatingly on the threshold of the Greek Letter Ranch-house. Lowell sneered openly.

"You haven't always been so tied up to your books that you couldn't get out," he said. "I want to take you back to a little horseback ride which you took just six weeks ago."

"I don't remember such a trip."

"You will remember it, as I particularize."

"Very well. You are beginning to interest me."

"You rode from here to the top of the hill on the Dollar Sign road. Do you remember?"

"What odds if I say yes or no? Go on. I want to hear the rest of this story."

"When you reached a clump of tall sage and grease wood, not far below the crest of the hill, you entered it and remained hidden. You had a considerable time to wait, but you were patient—very patient. You knew the man you wanted to meet was somewhere on the road—coming toward you. From the clump of bushes you commanded a view of the Dollar Sign road for miles. As I say, it was long and tedious waiting. It had rained in the night. The sun came out, strong and warm, and the atmosphere was moist. Your horse, that old white horse which has been on the ranch so many years, was impatiently fighting flies. Though you are not any kinder to horseflesh than you are to human beings who come within your blighting influence, you took the saddle off the animal. Perhaps the horse had caught his foot in a stirrup as he kicked at a buzzing fly."

The keen, strong features into which Lowell gazed were mask-like in their impassiveness.

"Soon you saw something approaching on the road over the prairie," went on the agent. "It must be the automobile driven by the man you had come to meet. You saddled quickly and rode out of the sagebrush. You met the man in the automobile as he was climbing the hill. He stopped and you talked with him. You had violent words, and then you shot him with a sawed-off shotgun which you had carried for that purpose. You killed the man, and then, to throw suspicion on others, conceived the idea of staking him down to the prairie. It would look like an Indian trick. Besides, you knew that there had been some trouble on the reservation with Indians who were dancing and generally inclined to oppose Government regulations. You had found a rope which had been dropped on the road by the half-breed, Jim McFann. You took that rope from your saddle and cut it in four pieces and tied the man's hands and wrists to his own tent-stakes, which you found in his automobile.

"Your plans worked out well. It was a lonely country and comparatively early in the day. There was nobody to disturb you at your work. Apparently you had thought of every detail. You had left a few tracks, and these you obliterated carefully. You knew you would hardly be suspected unless something led the world to your door. You had been a recluse for years, hated by white men and feared by red. Few had seen your face. You could retire to this lonely ranch and live your customary life, with no fear of suffering for the crime you had committed. To be sure, an Indian or two might be hanged, but a matter like that would rest lightly on your conscience.

"Apparently your plans were perfect, but you overlooked one small thing. Most clever scoundrels do. You did not think that perhaps Nature might lay a trap to catch you—a trap in the brush where you had been hidden. Your horse rolled in the mud to rid himself of the pest of flies. You were so intent on the approach of your victim that you did not notice the animal. Yet there in the mud, and visible to-day, was made the imprint of your horse's shoulder, *bearing the impression of the Greek Letter brand*!"

As Lowell finished, he rose slowly, his hands on the table and his gaze on the unflinching face in front of him. The gray-haired man rose also.

"I suppose," he said, in a voice from which all trace of harshness had disappeared, "you have come to give me over to the authorities on account of this crime."

"Yes."

"Very well. I committed the murder, much as you have explained it, but I did not ride the white horse to the hill. Nor am I Willis Morgan. I am Edward Sargent. Morgan was the man whom I killed and staked down on the prairie!"

CHAPTER XVI

Helen Ervin rode past the ranch door just as the gray-haired man made his statement to Lowell.

"You are Edward Sargent, the man who was supposed to have been murdered?" repeated the Indian agent, in astonishment.

"Yes; but wait till Miss Ervin comes in. The situation may require a little clearing, and she can help."

Surprise and anxiety alternated in Helen's face as she looked in through the open doorway and saw the men seated at the table. She paused a moment, silhouetted in the door, the Greek letter on the panel standing out with almost startling distinctness beside her. As she stood poised on the threshold in her riding-suit, the ravages of her previous trip having been repaired, she made Lowell think of a modernized Diana—modernized as to clothes, but carrying, in her straight-limbed grace, all the world-old spell of the outdoors.

"Our young friend has just learned the truth, my dear," said the gray-haired man. "He knows that I am Sargent, and that our stepfather, Willis Morgan, is dead."

Helen stepped quickly to Sargent's side. There was something suggesting filial protection in her attitude. Sargent smiled up at her, reassuringly.

"Probably it is better," he said, "that the whole thing should be known."

"But in a few days we should have been gone," said Helen. "Why have all our hopes been destroyed in this way at the last moment? Is this some of your work," she added bitterly, addressing Lowell—"some of your work as a spy?"

Sargent spoke up quickly.

"It was fate," he said. "I have felt from the first that I should not have attempted to escape punishment for my deed. The young man has simply done his duty. He worked with the sole idea of getting at the truth—and it is always the truth that matters most. What difference can it make who is hurt, so long as the truth is known?"

"But how did it become known," asked Helen, "when everything seemed to be so thoroughly in our favor? The innocent men who were suspected had been released. The public was content to let the crime rest at the door of Talpers—a man capable of any evil deed. What has happened to change matters so suddenly?"

"It was the old white horse that betrayed us," said Sargent, with a grim smile. "It shows on what small threads our fates hang balanced. The Greek letter brand still shows in the mud where the horse rolled on the day of the murder on the Dollar Sign hill. When our young friend here saw that bit of evidence, he came directly to the ranch and accused me of knowledge of the crime, all the time thinking I was Willis Morgan."

"Let me continue my work as a spy," broke in Lowell bitterly, "and ask for a complete statement."

"Willis Morgan was my twin brother," said Sargent. "As Willard Sargent he had made a distinguished name for himself among the teachers of Greek in this country. He was a professor at an early age, his bent toward scholarship being opposite to mine, which was along the lines of invention. My brother was a hard, cruel man, beneath a polished exterior. Cynicism was as natural to him as breathing. He married a young and beautiful woman, who had been married before, and who had a little daughter—a mere baby, Willard's wife soon died, a victim of his cynicism and studied cruelty. The future of this helpless stepdaughter of my brother's became a matter of the most intimate concern to me. My brother was mercenary to a marked degree. I had become successful in my inventions of mining machinery. I was fast making a fortune. Willard called upon me frequently for loans, which I never refused. In fact, I had voluntarily advanced him thousands of dollars, from which I expected no return. A mere brotherly feeling of gratitude would have been sufficient repayment for me. But such a feeling my brother never had. His only object was to get as much out of me as he could, and to sneer at me, in his high-bred way, while making a victim of me.

"His success in getting money from me led him into deep waters. He victimized others, who threatened prosecution. Realizing that matters could not go on as they were going, I told my brother that I would take up the claims against him and give him one hundred thousand dollars, on certain conditions. Those conditions were that he was to renounce all claim to his little stepdaughter, and that I was to have sole care of her. He was to go to some distant part of the country and change his name and let the world forget that such a creature as Willard Sargent ever existed.

"My brother was forced to agree to the terms laid down. The university trustees were threatening him with expulsion. He resigned and came out here. He married an Indian woman, and, as I understand it, killed her by the same cold-hearted, deliberately cruel treatment that had brought about the death of his first wife.

"Meantime Willard's stepdaughter, who was none other than Helen, was brought up by a lifelong friend of mine, Miss Scovill, at her school for girls in California. The loving care that she was given can best be told by Helen. I did not wish the girl to know that she was dependent upon her uncle for support. In fact, I did not want her to learn anything which might lead to inquiries into her babyhood, and which would only bring her sorrow when she learned of her mother's fate. My brother, always clever in his rascalities, learned that Helen knew nothing of my existence. He sent her a letter, when Miss Scovill was away, telling Helen that he had been crippling himself financially to keep her in school, and now he needed her at this ranch. Before Miss Scovill had returned, Helen, acting on the impulse of the moment, had departed for my brother's place. Miss Scovill was greatly alarmed, and sent me a telegram. As soon as I received word, I started for my brother's ranch. I happened to have started on an automobile tour at the time, and figured that I could reach here as quickly by machine as by making frequent changes from rail to stage.

"When Helen arrived at the ranch, it can be imagined how the success of his scheme delighted Willis Morgan, as my brother was known here. He threatened her with the direst of evils, and declared he would drag her beneath the level of the poorest squaw on the Indian reservation. Fortunately she is a girl of spirit and determination. The Chinese servant was willing to help her to escape. She would have fled at the first opportunity, in spite of my brother's declaration that escape would be impossible, but it happened that, during the course of his boasting, her captor overstepped himself. He told her of my existence, and that I had really been the one who had kept her in school. He had managed to keep a thorough system of espionage in effect, so far as Miss Scovill and myself were concerned. He had known when she left San Francisco, and he also knew that I was coming, by automobile, to take Helen from the ranch. He laughed as he told her of my coming. All the ferocity of his nature blazed forth, and he told Helen that he intended to kill me at sight, and would also kill her.

"Desirous of warning me, even at risk of her own life, Helen mailed a letter to me at Quaking-Asp Grove, hoping to catch me before I reached that place. In this letter she warned me not to come to the ranch, as she felt that tragedy impended. Talpers held up the letter and read it, and thought to hold it as a club over Helen's head, showing that she knew something of the murder.

"I rode through Quaking-Asp Grove and White Lodge and the Indian agency at night. I had a breakdown after going past Talpers's store—a tire to replace. By the time I climbed the hill on the Dollar Sign road it was well along in the morning. I saw a man coming toward me on a white horse. It was my brother, Willard Sargent, or Willis Morgan. He looked much like me. The years seemed to have dealt with us about alike. I knew, as soon as I saw him, that he had come out to kill me. We talked a few minutes. I had stopped the car at his demand, and he sat in the saddle, close beside me. There is no need of going into the details of our conversation. He was full of reproaches. His later life had been more of a punishment for him than I had suspected. His voice was full of venom as he threatened me. He told me that Helen was at the ranch, but I would never see her. He had a sawed-off shotgun in his hand. I had no weapon. I made a quick leap at him and threw him from his horse. The shotgun fell in the road. I jumped for it just as he scrambled after it. I wrested the weapon from him. He tried to draw a revolver that swung in a holster at his hip. There was no chance for me to take that from him. It was a case of his life or mine. I fired the shotgun, and the charge tore away the lower part of his face.

"Strangely enough, I had no regret at what I had done. It was not that I had saved my own life—I had managed to intervene between Helen and a fate worse than death. I weighed matters and acted with a coolness that surprised me, even while I was carrying out the details that followed. It occurred to me that, because of our close resemblance to each other, it might be possible for me to pass myself off as my brother. I knew that he had lived the life of a recluse here, and that few people knew him by sight. We were dressed much alike, as I was traveling in khaki, and he wore clothes of that material. I removed everything from his pockets, and then I put my watch and checkbook and other papers in his pockets. I even went so far as to put my wallet in his inner pocket, containing bills of large denomination.

"I had heard that there was some dissatisfaction among certain young Indians on the reservation—that those Indians were dancing and making trouble in general. It seemed to me that such a situation might be made use of in some way. Why not drag my brother's body out on the prairie at the side of the road and stake it down? Suspicion might be thrown on the Indians. I had no sooner thought of the plan than I proceeded to carry it out. I worked calmly and quickly. There was no living thing in sight to cause alarm. I took a rawhide lariat, which I found attached to the saddle on the old white horse, and used it to tie my brother's ankles and wrists to tent-stakes which I took from my automobile.

"After my work was done, I looked it over carefully, to see that I had left nothing undone and had made no blunder in what I had accomplished. I obliterated all tracks, as far as possible. Although it had rained the night before, and there was mud in the old buffalo wallows and in the depressions in the road, the prairie where I had staked the body was dry and dusty.

"After I had arranged everything to my satisfaction, I mounted the old white horse and rode to the ranch, merely following the trail the horse had made coming out. When I arrived here and made myself known to Helen, you can imagine her joy, which soon was changed to consternation when she found what had been done. But my plan of living here and letting the world suppose that I was Willard Sargent, or Willis Morgan, seemed feasible. Wong was our friend from the first. We knew we could depend on his Oriental discretion. But we were not to escape lightly. Talpers's attitude was a menace until, through a fortunate set of circumstances, we managed to secure a compensating hold over him. Undoubtedly Talpers had been first on the scene after the murder. He had robbed my brother's body, and was caught in his ghoul-like act by his partner, Jim McFann. The half-breed believed Talpers when the trader told him that a watch was all he had found on the dead man. The later discovery that Talpers had deceived him, and had really taken a large sum of money from the body, led the half-breed to kill the trader.

"I decided to await the outcome of the trial. It would have been impossible for me to let Fire Bear or McFann go to prison, or perhaps to the gallows, for my deed. If either one, or both, had been convicted, I intended to make a confession. But matters seemed to work out well for us. The accused men were freed, and it seemed to be the general opinion that Talpers had committed the crime. Talpers was dead. There was no occasion for me to confess. I had thoughts of going away, quietly, to some place where I could begin life over again. Miss Scovill is in possession of a will making Helen my heir. This will could have been produced, and thus Helen would have been well provided for. I had kept in seclusion here, and had even feigned illness, in order that none might suspect me of being other than Willis Morgan. But if any one had seen me I do not believe the deception would have been discovered, so close is my resemblance to my brother. Always having been a passable mimic, I imitated my brother's voice. It was a voice that had often stirred me to wrath, because of its cold, cutting qualities. The first time I imitated my brother's voice, Wong came in from the kitchen looking frightened beyond measure. He thought the ghost of his old employer had returned to the ranch.

"But of what use is all such planning when destiny wills otherwise? A trifling incident—the rolling of a horse in the mud—brought everything about my ears. Yet I believe it is for the best. Nor do I believe your discovery to have been a mere matter of chance. Probably you were led by a higher force than mere devotion to duty. Truth must have loyal servitors such as you if justice is to survive in this world. I am heartily glad that you persisted in your search. I feel more at ease in mind and body to-night than I have felt since the day of the tragedy. Now if you will excuse me a moment, I will make preparations for giving myself up to the authorities—perhaps to higher authorities than those at White Lodge."

Sargent stepped into the adjoining room as he finished talking. Helen did not raise her head from the table. Something in Sargent's final words roused Lowell's suspicion. He walked quickly into the room and found Sargent taking a revolver from the drawer of a desk. Lowell wrested the weapon from his grasp.

"That's the last thing in the world you should do," said the Indian agent, in a low voice. "There isn't a jury that will convict you. If it's expiation you seek, do you think that cowardly sort of expiation is going to bring anything but new unhappiness to *her* out there?"

"No," said Sargent. "I give you my word this will not be attempted again."

Space meeting space—plains and sky welded into harmonies of blue and gray. Cloud shadows racing across billowy uplands, and sagebrush nodding in a breeze crisp and electric as only a breeze from our upper Western plateau can be. Distant mountains, with their allurements enhanced by the filmiest of purple veils. Bird song and the chattering of prairie dogs from the foreground merely intensifying the great, echoless silence of the plains.

Lowell and Helen from a ridge—*their* ridge it was now!—watched the changes of the panorama. They had dismounted, and their horses were standing near at hand, reins trailing, and manes rising and falling with the undulations of the breeze. It was a month after Sargent's confession and his surrender as the slayer of the recluse of the Greek Letter Ranch. As Lowell had prophesied, Sargent's acquittal had been prompt. His story was corroborated by brief testimony from Lowell and Helen. Citizens crowded about him, after the jury had brought in its verdict of "Not guilty," and one of the first to congratulate him was Jim McFann, who had been acquitted when he came up for trial for slaying Talpers. The half-breed told Sargent of Talpers's plan to kill Helen.

"I'm just telling you," said the half-breed, "to ease your mind in case you're feeling any responsibility for Talpers's death."

Soon after his acquittal Sargent departed for California, where he married Miss Scovill—the outcome of an early romance. Helen was soon to leave to join her foster parents, and she and Lowell had come for a last ride.

"I cannot realize the glorious truth of it all—that I am to come soon and claim you and bring you back here as my wife," said Lowell. "Say it all over again for me."

He was standing with both arms about her and with her face uptilted to his. No doubt other men and women had stood thus on this glacier-wrought promontory—lovers from cave and tepee.

"It is all true," Helen answered, "but I must admit that the responsibilities of being an Indian agent's wife seem alarming. The thought of there being so much to do among these people makes me afraid that I shall not be able to meet the responsibilities."

"You'll be bothered every day with Indians—men, women, and babies. You'll hear the thumping of their moccasined feet every hour of the day. They'll overrun your front porch and seek you out in the sacred precincts of your kitchen, mostly about things that are totally inconsequential."

"But think of the work in its larger aspects—the good that there is to be done."

Lowell smiled at her approvingly.

"That's the way you have to keep thinking all the time. You have to look beyond the mass of detail in the foreground—past all the minor annoyances and the red tape and the seeming ingratitude. You've got to figure that you're there to supply the needed human note—to let these people understand that this Government of ours is not a mere machine with the motive power at Washington. You've got to feel that you've been sent here to make up for the indifference of the outside world—that the kiddies out in those ramshackle cabins and cold tepees are not going to be lonely, and suffer and die, if you can help it. You've got to feel that it's your help that's going to save the feeble and sick—sometimes from their own superstitions. There's no reason why we can't in time get a hospital here for Indians, like Fire Bear, who have tuberculosis. We're going to save Fire Bear, and we can save others. And then there are the school-children, with lonely hours that can be lightened, and with work to be found for them in the big world after they have learned the white man's tasks. But there are going to be heartaches and disillusionments for a woman. A man can grit his teeth and smash through some way, unless he sinks back into absolute indifference as a good many Indian agents do. But a woman—well, dear, I dread to think of your embarking on a task which is at once so alluring and so endless and thankless."

Helen put her hand on his lips.

"With you helping me, no task can seem thankless."

"Well, then, this is our kingdom of work," said Lowell, with a sweep of his sombrero which included the vast reservation which smiled so inscrutably at them. "There's every human need to be met out there in all that bigness. We'll face it together—and we'll win!"

They rode back leisurely along the ridge and took the trail that led to the ranch. The house was closed, as Wong was at the agency, ready to leave for the Sargents' place in California. The old white horse, which Helen rode, tried to turn in at the ranch gate.

"The poor old fellow doesn't understand that his new home is at the agency," said Helen. "He is the only one that wants to return to this place of horrors."

"The leasers will be here soon," replied Lowell. "They are going to put up buildings and make a new place all told. The Greek letter on the door will be gone, but, no matter what changes are made, I have no doubt that people will continue to know it as Mystery Ranch."